She wanted him—loved being in his arms.

She longed to have him tell her the things she wanted to hear, but how could that ever come about? He didn't love her, did he? He'd never said those words she desperately needed him to say. And through it all he was still her boss—the man who held power over her future. Hadn't she told herself she would never get into this situation ever again? What was wrong with her that she couldn't find the will-power to keep him at arm's length?

Dear Reader

Islands hold a special place in most people's hearts, I would imagine. The idea of love blossoming on a palm-fringed paradise is wonderfully romantic, and conjures up all kinds of possibilities.

But things may not always be what they seem. Living and working on an island comes with its own set of problems—as my heroine soon begins to find out.

I had a great time seeing how Saskia managed to contend with all her difficulties—Tyler being first and foremost among them. Falling for the boss was never going to be a good idea as far as she was concerned, and the fact that they were total opposites added a whole other dimension to her troubles.

I hope you, too, enjoy the journey as Tyler and Saskia work together to find a solution to their problems.

Love

Joanna

DARING TO
DATE HER BOSS

BY
JOANNA NEIL

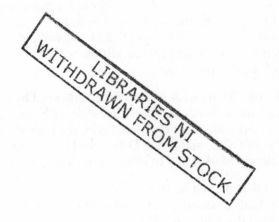

MILLS
BOON

Published in Great Britain 2014
by Mills & Boon, an imprint of Harlequin (UK) Limited,
Large Print edition 2015
Eton House, 18-24 Paradise Road,
Richmond, Surrey, TW9 1SR

© 2014 Joanna Neil

ISBN: 978-0-263-25460-0

Printed and bound in Great Britain
by CPI Antony Rowe, Chippenham, Wiltshire

When **Joanna Neil** discovered Mills & Boon®, her lifelong addiction to reading crystallised into an exciting new career writing Mills & Boon® Medical Romance™. Her characters are probably the outcome of her varied lifestyle, which includes working as a clerk, typist, nurse and infant teacher. She enjoys dressmaking and cooking at her Leicestershire home. Her family includes a husband, son and daughter, an exuberant yellow Labrador and two slightly crazed cockatiels. She currently works with a team of tutors at her local education centre, to provide creative writing workshops for people interested in exploring their own writing ambitions.

Recent titles by Joanna Neil:

A DOCTOR TO REMEMBER
SHELTERED BY HER TOP-NOTCH BOSS
RETURN OF THE REBEL DOCTOR
HIS BRIDE IN PARADISE
TAMED BY HER BROODING BOSS
DR RIGHT ALL ALONG
DR LANGLEY: PROTECTOR OR PLAYBOY?
A COTSWOLD CHRISTMAS BRIDE
THE TAMING OF DR ALEX DRAYCOTT
BECOMING DR BELLINI'S BRIDE

These books are also available in eBook format from www.millsandboon.co.uk

CHAPTER ONE

'DROP IT, BOOMER. Right now. Drop it and give it back.'

Saskia turned over in bed and pulled the duvet more closely around her. What was going on? Why was there so much noise? Dimly, her sleep-befuddled brain made out eight-year-old Becky's voice, growing shrill with urgency. Saskia blinked, and drowsily stretched her limbs before opening her eyes a fraction. She peered groggily around the unfamiliar room.

Soft sunlight filtered through the chenille curtains, highlighting the glazed, Georgian-style wardrobe doors and the wide dressing table with its plush upholstered stool. It was a lovely room, but for a moment or two Saskia stared at it, perplexed. What was she was doing here? And what on earth was all the shouting about? She was used to peaceful mornings, to gradually waking to the low sound of the radio on her bedside table. There was no such luck today.

A loud wail shocked her into sitting upright. Groaning softly, she swung her legs out from under the cosy duvet and rested her bare feet on the carpeted floor. What time was it?

She reached for the short silk robe that was draped over a nearby chair. Pulling it on over her thigh-length nightshirt, it was all starting to come back to her. Her circumstances had changed pretty dramatically over the past few days. She was here to look after the children. A small wave of panic engulfed her. In that case, what was she doing in bed while they were up and about?

'You're a bad dog, Boomer. I don't like you any more. Go away.'

There was a sharp tap on the bedroom door and Saskia must have muttered acknowledgement because two seconds later the door was flung open and an irate Becky stood in front of her, angry tears staining her flushed cheeks.

'Boomer's chewed Milly's bottle and now it's ruined—look.' The child thrust the offending object towards her, and Saskia gazed blearily at what had once been a doll's feeding bottle. Becky was right. It was ruined, that was for sure.

Saskia put a comforting arm around her niece's shoulders and laid her head against the child's golden curls. 'I'm sure we'll manage to get another one for you next time we go to the shops. You have to keep these things out of Boomer's way, you know. He might be two years old, but he still acts like a pup a lot of the time.'

'Well, he's a bad dog.'

'Yes.' Straightening, she glanced at the watch on her bedside table. It was ten o'clock already? Another quiver of alarm washed through her until she remembered that she didn't have a job to go to and, anyway, it was Saturday. So…no worries there, were there? Hah. As if.

The doorbell rang a couple of minutes later as she wandered into the living room to check that all was well with Becky's brother and sister. Boomer, the family's exuberant springer spaniel, set up a frantic barking in response to the door chimes, and Saskia frowned. Her head was beginning to ache.

Who could that be? She really wasn't in the mood for visitors. Besides, the place was a mess, with packing crates everywhere and half-opened boxes taking up every available surface.

Six-year-old Charlie was trailing his cars over the play mat in a corner of the room and acknowledged her with an absent 'Hiya' as she greeted him with a smile.

Seeing her, Boomer stopped barking and raced up to her, wagging his tail and almost knocking her over in his excitement. She patted his silky, chocolate-coloured fur as she glanced around. Caitlin was nowhere to be seen. Most likely she was still tucked up in bed, like teenagers everywhere. The thought filled her with envy.

'Perhaps you should come in,' she heard Becky saying cautiously. 'My mummy isn't here, but you can talk to my auntie if you like.'

Saskia immediately tensed and hurried out of the room and into the hallway, ready to avert disaster. She wasn't dressed properly—how could she possibly meet up with anyone while she was in this state?

But she was already too late…a man carrying a large package, a box of some sort, was following Becky down the hallway towards the living room.

For a second or two, as she studied him, Saskia's breath caught in her throat. He was in his mid-thirties, she guessed, and he was absolutely stunning…long, lean and incredibly fit looking, dressed in smart casuals, a dark, open-neck shirt and cream-coloured trousers. She closed her eyes briefly to savour the moment. Wow! So this was what the Isles of Scilly had to offer.

His jet-black hair was cut in a short, crisp style that perfectly suited his angular features. As to his eyes—well, his stunning blue gaze was mesmerising, except that right now it was directed at her, bringing warm colour flooding to her cheeks as she realised she'd been caught staring at him.

But he, too, seemed to have been knocked off balance by their unexpected meeting. She heard the sharp intake of his breath and saw his eyes widen as his glance moved over her in turn, taking in every softly feminine curve. He was suddenly rooted to the spot, his gaze sweeping like a lick of flame over the smooth expanse of legs that were lightly bronzed from a summer of sunshine.

A sudden arc of electric tension sparked between them, an intense, sensual intimacy that brought with it a wave of heat that raced through her body. She couldn't move, didn't know how to go on.

Then the stranger made a rough-edged, broken kind of sound, as though he meant to say something but instead the words seemed to choke in his throat.

Coming to her senses, Saskia tugged awkwardly at the hem of her robe, trying to cover a bit more thigh, an action that only resulted in drawing the edges of the garment further apart. Taking a deep breath, she wrapped the silk more firmly around herself and tied the belt in what she hoped was a secure knot.

'I—uh…' He hesitated, drawing his gaze back to her face. Like her, he seemed to be struggling to get himself back together. 'I um…I gather you're not Mrs Reynolds…'

'Er, no, I'm her sister-in-law…Saskia.'

'Ah, I see.' He nodded acknowledgment, then pulled in a deep breath and straightened his shoulders. 'I'm Tyler, Tyler Beckett. I have a parcel for Mrs Reynolds.' He indicated the large box he was carrying, marked *'Glass, Handle with Care'*. 'I've been hanging onto it for a couple of days, ever since the courier dropped it off next door.'

'Oh…thanks.' Her breathing had settled

down at last to a heavy thud and now her brow furrowed. 'My brother said something about Megan ordering a new light fitting…I guess this must be it. He said she'd checked with the landlord to make sure it would be okay to change things.'

'Yes, I told her I'm okay with it, as long as she runs things by me first.'

He was the landlord? That came as a bit of a surprise. She went to take the box from him but he hesitated, saying, 'Actually, this is quite heavy. Maybe it would be better if I put it down for you, somewhere safe?'

'Oh…yes, of course.' She studied him surreptitiously. This could be difficult. If he owned the place, how was he going to react to seeing what had happened to his once pristine property now that three children and a dog had cut a swathe through it? There was already a scuff mark on the wall where Charlie had run amok.

He was watching her expectantly and she galvanised herself into action. Fighting back a nervous quiver of apprehension, she showed him into the L-shaped living room, padding barefoot across the smooth oak floorboards to the dining area. 'You could put it down here, if you like.'

To her shame, there were four dirty soup bowls on the table, the remnants of last night's hastily prepared supper. She'd been too tired to clear away after the meal and, besides, she'd figured it was more important to try to sort out the childcare arrangements, or at least find out what her options were. She still had to see if there was anyone around who would be prepared to walk the dog—if she managed to find a job it would be unfair to leave Boomer cooped up at home all day.

She quickly moved the crockery out of the way, along with a jumble of household ornaments, and waved a hand towards the clear space on the large, solid wood table.

Her brother had rented the house partly furnished and she was impressed—from what she'd seen so far, his new landlord certainly had an eye for quality.

At the moment, though, he was looking around, a bewildered expression on his face as he took in the chaos. Charlie had spread his toys generously around the room—his was the first box that had been opened as he'd been desperate to be reunited with his belongings, and Saskia had been anxious to keep him occupied. Next in line had been Boomer's collection of chew toys—a couple of facsimile bones, a rubber ring, a pull toy made of knotted strings and his favourite, a plastic, squashy ball. They, too, were strewn across the floor.

Tyler frowned, absorbing everything in that one glance, and Saskia winced. She wondered if he was familiar with the mayhem of family life. The slight bracing of his shoulders seemed a dead giveaway.

Still, he didn't comment. 'I was busy at work the last couple of days,' he said, as he set down the parcel, 'and I could see you were dealing with the removal van until late in the evening yesterday, so I didn't like to disturb you.'

'That was thoughtful of you,' she murmured,

leaning forward to help with the positioning of the parcel and faltering a little when she realised he was running his gaze over her once more. Heat flickered in his smoke-dark eyes as he took in the cloud of coppery curls that framed her oval face and brushed against the creamy slope of her shoulders.

Belatedly, she realised that her shoulder was indeed bare, and she quickly tugged her robe back in place. The wide neckline of her night-shirt had somehow managed to slide partway down over her arms.

'I…um…I should apologise for being dressed like this…only you caught me unawares. I overslept. It's not something I do regularly,' she added hastily, 'it's just that…uh…' It was just that she'd been up half the night, using her laptop to sort out the route to school and trying to find suitable day care for the children after school and a whole host of other things he didn't need to know about. Doing it when the children were tucked up in bed had seemed like the best opportunity. 'We did a lot of travelling on Thursday to get here. Then there were two and a half hours on the ferry and the journey from where we docked to here. And we don't seem to have stopped since. I haven't caught up with myself yet.'

'It's all right. You don't have to explain yourself.' His expression was wry, and she could guess what he was thinking. She'd already burned her boats on that one.

She started to move away from the table and his glance slid down to her bare feet, lingering there as though he'd only just noticed her toenails were painted a shimmering, luscious pink. He seemed intrigued, curious even, and he certainly didn't seem to be in any hurry to leave, leading her to wonder uncomfortably if she ought to offer him coffee. It would be the neighbourly thing to do, wouldn't it?

'Um…can I offer you—?' She broke off as Boomer, abandoning his knotted pull toy, bounded up to her once more and joyfully nudged her hip, tipping her off balance.

Reacting swiftly, Tyler put out his arms to steady her. 'You were saying…?'

'Oh, yes…um…' It was totally distracting, having him stand so close to her, and for some reason it took a real effort to unscramble her brain. His hands lightly circled her arms, sending small eddies of warmth throughout her body. While he was holding her like this she simply couldn't think straight.

'Coffee,' she said at last. 'I was going to offer you coffee.'

'Thanks, I'd like that.' He released her and she let out a long, silent breath of relief. 'You can perhaps fill me in on one or two things,' he added, 'like what's happening with your brother and his wife.'

She nodded, but a quiver of anguish rippled through her. That wasn't going to be easy to recount, was it, with Sam and Megan both in hospital and neither of them likely to recover very soon? As their landlord, she supposed he had a right to know, but it was hard for her to talk about it. Coming out of the blue on a busy road, the accident had shocked all of them.

Boomer followed them into the kitchen, still nudging her gently, as though anxious that she should head in the right direction, and it dawned on her that he must be eager for his breakfast. 'Okay, Boomer,' she told him. 'I'll feed you. Just give me a minute.'

Caitlin had finally put in an appearance and was sitting at the round table in one corner of the room, her mid-brown hair falling across her cheek like a curtain as she hunched over her mobile phone. 'He's used to being fed at eight o'clock,' the teenager remarked, a faint note of censure in her voice as Saskia emptied kibble into Boomer's food bowl. The girl tossed her hair out of the way with a shake of her head. 'You were late with his meals yesterday as well, and the day before that.'

'Well, we've had a lot going on over the last few days,' Saskia defended herself, uneasily conscious of Tyler showing an interest in the conversation. 'I'll be much more organised once I get the hang of things.'

'Yeah, right. It'll probably be better if I take over feeding him.' Caitlin sighed and pushed a half-eaten bowl of dry cereal towards Saskia. 'I can't eat that. Mum always buys the proper branded version.' She pressed her lips into a flat, disgruntled line. 'And Charlie's finished off all the milk again.'

'Oh, dear.' Saskia frowned. As well as being upset about what had happened to her parents, Caitlin, at fourteen, was going through a definite grumpy phase.

Tyler intervened. 'Don't worry about coffee. It doesn't matter.'

She shook her head. 'I have some sachets somewhere. We even have a choice—latte or cappuccino. I think you'll like them.' Her gaze travelled around the room, searching for the box where they were packed, and after a moment or two she realised that he was looking with her.

'There are quite a few boxes to choose from,

aren't there?' His gaze settled on a collection of crockery and cookery books that were spread out over the worktop and slowly his eyes half closed as he though he was trying to shut out this alien world he'd stumbled into.

'No, it's okay, they're in the cupboard,' Saskia said in triumph. 'I remember I put them where they would be near to the kettle. Yay!' She hurried forward to retrieve them at the same time that Boomer came and dropped his ball in front of her and then gazed at her in panting anticipation.

'Ow, ow, ow...' She yelped in pain as she stepped on one of his plastic chew toys and began to hop around the tiled floor, clutching her foot.

'What's wrong?' Caitlin asked, getting up from her seat to come and look. Then, 'Oh... that's blood,' she said in an anxious voice. 'You're bleeding, Sass.' She inspected the hard nylon, bone-shaped toy. 'It's really rough around the edges where he's been having a go at it. Are you going to be all right?'

Saskia pulled in a deep breath. 'Of course I am.' She stopped hopping and gingerly put her foot to the floor. 'I'll be fine. Don't worry.' The last thing she needed was for the children to be concerned about her. They had enough on their plates right now. Instead, she flicked the switch on the kettle and tried to ignore the stinging in her foot, busying herself adding coffee powder to a couple of mugs.

'I don't suppose you have a first-aid kit to hand, do you?' Tyler asked, and Saskia thought about it then shook her head.

'I recall seeing it somewhere.' She frowned.

'I'll go and fetch mine.'

'There's no need, really. I'll be fine.'

He gave her an assessing look. 'You won't be if you go on the way you're doing now. Sit down and stop spreading blood over the floor. You don't want to get an infection, do you?'

'N-no, of course not.'

'Good. Then sit down and wait there until I get back.'

After he'd gone, Caitlin finished making the

coffees and then studied the chew toy once more. 'I'm going to put this in the bin,' she said. 'Maybe Boomer should go out in the garden and get some fresh air. He has way too much energy.'

'That's a good idea. Perhaps Charlie would like to play with him out there? Anyway, he and Becky need to go and feed their rabbit.'

'Yeah, I'll tell them as soon as I've cleaned up the floor.'

Saskia smiled at her. 'Thanks, Caitlin. You're a treasure.'

Tyler was back within a couple of minutes. Noticing that Boomer was nowhere to be seen, he glanced out of the kitchen window and saw that the dog was racing around outside, having a whale of a time with the two younger children.

Hearing their laughter, Saskia guessed Becky must have forgiven Boomer for his earlier misdemeanour.

Tyler placed a fresh carton of milk in the

fridge and then set out a fully equipped medical pack on the kitchen table.

'I guess that's the flower border done for,' he murmured on a rueful note, glancing out of the window once more as he went over to the sink and poured warm water into a bowl.

'I'm really sorry about all this,' Saskia said. She waved a hand towards his coffee mug. 'Please, help yourself.' Perhaps a reviving drink would help him to feel better.

'Thanks.' He went on setting out his equipment.

Saskia bit her lip. 'Maybe I could put some sort of decorative fencing up to keep him away from the plants.' She frowned. 'You've caught us at a bad time, but we planned on getting to grips with everything today—well, over the weekend, at least. Caitlin's just gone to start unpacking clothes and to put things right upstairs.'

He nodded, drawing up a chair in front of her and laying a towel over the seat. 'Rest your leg on there. I'm going to bathe your foot first to make sure there are no bits of debris in the wound.'

'Okay…thanks.' She watched him as he hunkered down and began to work. He was very thorough, cleaning her foot with meticulous care and then gently drying it.

'There are several small puncture wounds,' he commented. 'I'll press some gauze against it for a while until the bleeding stops.'

'You look as though you've done this sort of thing before,' she murmured, looking over his medical pack with interest.

'I have, although I usually have to deal with rather more serious injuries than this,' he answered soberly. 'I'm a doctor. I work at the hospital on the island, in the emergency department, and I'm on the rota as a first attender where the paramedics need a doctor to go along and help out.'

'Ah, that explains it,' she said, speaking half to herself.

'I beg your pardon?' He glanced at her, absently resting his hand lightly on her leg before pausing to check under the gauze to see if the bleeding had stopped.

She cleared her throat. His touch was doing very strange things to her nervous system. Things she'd thought she'd long forgotten. 'It's just that you have that kind of air about you,' she explained, 'as though you're very capable, well organised, and know exactly what has to be done. I expect seeing the state we're in here has been a bit of a shock for you.'

He didn't answer, but his mouth moved in a faint curve. He applied a topical antiseptic and then bound up her foot, securing the neat bandage with tape.

'That should be a bit more comfortable for you,' he said. Finally, he stood up, reaching for his coffee and taking a long swallow. He paused for a moment, staring at his cup in puzzlement, and she guessed he was faintly surprised to discover that he quite liked the taste. 'So how do you fit into the picture here?' he asked. 'Did you decide to move over here with your brother and his family, or were you already living on the island?'

'Uh, I came over here when my brother and his wife were…delayed.' She still didn't want to talk about what had happened and hoped he wouldn't persist. 'I have to get the children into school for the new term, and of course the removal had been planned and booked a few weeks ahead. It was important that things went smoothly.'

He nodded. 'What do you think of our island? Have you been here before?'

She shook her head, making the silky, copper curls quiver and dance. 'I saw it for the first time on Thursday. It's so beautiful, it took my breath away—the lovely beaches and the clear blue water, the palm trees… It's like a subtropical paradise.'

His mouth curved. 'Yes, it is.' He stood up and started to clear away his equipment just as the kitchen door burst open and Charlie came rushing in.

'Boomer's been sick all over the flowers,' he

announced. 'It's yucky. He's brought up all of his breakfast and there's lots of grass in it, too.'

Saskia groaned. 'Did you let him out into the garden first thing this morning?'

'Becky did.'

She sighed. 'That must have been when he did it. We'll have to stop him eating grass somehow.' She looked at Charlie. 'Okay, I'll come and hose it down in a bit. Try to stop him from running around, will you, but keep him out there for a bit longer if you can until his stomach settles down?'

'Okay.' Charlie went outside once more and Tyler sent her a brief, sympathetic glance.

'I'd better leave you to get on. It looks as though you have your hands full.'

She nodded, giving him a regretful look. 'Like I said, it should all be sorted out over the weekend.'

She stood up, testing her foot against the hard floor. 'That feels good,' she said. 'It must be all the padding you put in there. Thank you so much for helping me out. And thanks for the milk—I appreciate it. You'll have earned your-self a thousand brownie points with Caitlin.'

He smiled. 'You're welcome.' He left by the kitchen door, and she heard him saying good-bye to the children as he left. As she glanced out of the window, she saw him briefly pat Boomer on the head.

She looked disconsolately at the mess around her. There couldn't have been a worse time for the landlord to pay them a visit, but that wasn't the worst of it, was it? They shared the same profession. She was a doctor, too. How would it be if he heard about her application for a job at the hospital where he worked? She couldn't see that going down too well.

For all that he'd been pleasant to her and he had helped her out, she suspected that he didn't think very much of her lackadaisical ways. There was no point suggesting that she would put everything right…she had a strong feel-ing that, left to him, he would have organised things properly from the start, and everyone, probably even the dog, would have been given a job to do to help out.

Still, she couldn't help wishing things had been different. After all, he was the kind of man women dreamed of, and she was by no means immune...even though she'd sworn off men. He'd made her body tingle just by being near... And when he'd rested his hand on her bare leg...phew.

She sighed. Maybe it was just as well she'd made a bad impression on him. It would nip things in the bud from the outset...because she really ought to have learned her lesson by now. After all, it was only when you got to know men that things started to go wrong.

CHAPTER TWO

'CHARLIE, WILL YOU hurry up, please? We need to get a move on or we'll be late.'

Saskia looked around the kitchen, mentally ticking off a list in her head. 'Becky, don't forget your PE kit—you need to take that with you as well as your backpack.'

'Yeah, okay.'

'Do you have everything you need, Caitlin?' She peered into the hallway to look at the teenager, who was frowning at her hair in the mirror and trying to brush loose strands into place, something she'd been doing for the last several minutes. 'What about your geometry set—did you remember to put it in your bag? Perhaps I should have a quick look, just to make sure.'

Caitlin whipped the backpack away from her before Saskia had a chance to investigate. 'I can sort my own things out,' she said, turning away and pressing a hand against her forehead as though her head was aching. 'I don't need anyone checking up on me.'

Saskia winced. So far, nothing was going to plan. Her vision of a smooth, hassle-free morning getting ready for this first day of the school term was dissolving with every minute that passed. Caitlin had been tetchy ever since she'd dragged herself out of bed, and when you added in Becky's insistence on taking time to go outside to pet her lop-eared rabbit, and Charlie's complete oblivion to everything going on around him, getting them all organised and ready was rapidly turning into a stressful situation.

'Charlie, can you switch off that computer game? We're leaving right now.'

It must be great for Tyler next door to simply ease himself into his sleek, shining BMW and head off for the hospital without a care in the world. She'd seen him leave his house about half an hour ago, perfectly groomed, dressed in an immaculate dark suit, his hair crisply styled. She'd caught the glint of a cufflink as he'd reached to open the car door. His whole life was probably streamlined.

She shepherded everyone towards the front door, but as they were about to leave Becky said urgently, 'Saskia—wait. I think Boomer's being sick in the kitchen. I can hear him.' The little girl went back in there to take a closer look. 'Yeuw! It's got lots of bits of tissue in it.'

Saskia sighed. Tyler certainly never had to deal with anything like this, did he? She looked at Charlie. 'Have you been feeding Boomer paper towels again?'

He shook his head vigorously, but she noticed he couldn't quite meet her eyes.

'It's bad for him,' she said firmly. 'And it's not helping us either, because now I have to stop and clean up after him when we're already pushed for time. Perhaps you'd better come and give me a hand. Go and let him outside in case he needs to be sick some more.'

A few minutes later she settled Boomer down

in his bed in the kitchen and they finally started out on the walk to school. It was a good thing the primary and secondary schools were on the same site, Saskia reflected. At least it made things a little easier.

Of all the mornings to be delayed, this was the worst, because as soon as she had dropped off the children she was supposed to go for her interview at the hospital. She really needed that job, and she was more than a little anxious about it. In fact, she was beginning to feel quite apprehensive. There was money coming in from her brother's bank account to pay the rent, but now she had three extra mouths to feed and the bills were mounting up. Her savings would only take her so far.

Arriving at the school a few minutes later, she gave Becky and Charlie a hug and told a still fractious Caitlin she hoped she'd have a good day. She would have hugged her, too, but the teenager made it clear she didn't want any demonstration of affection, especially not in front of the other students.

She was about to leave when someone said, 'Ah, Miss Reynolds—or should I call you Dr Reynolds? I saw you helping Charlie to find his peg in the cloakroom a little while ago and realised you must be the newcomers to our school.'

Saskia glanced at the woman who had approached her. She was tall, with medium-length dark hair cut in a stylish bob, and there was an undeniable look of authority about her. 'Hello. Yes, that's right. I'm Dr Reynolds.'

The woman smiled. 'I'm Elizabeth Hunter, the headmistress—I'm so glad I managed to meet up with you.' She was keen to talk to Saskia about the children's parents and how their accident might have affected the youngsters. 'We want to be as supportive as possible,' she said.

'Thank you. I appreciate that. It has been a difficult time for them, but I'm hoping that if we let the children talk about their worries it might help.' Saskia spoke to the headmistress for a few minutes, wanting to ease the children's transition into their new school as best she could but conscious all the while that the clock was ticking and she needed to get away to the hospital.

At last, though, she was free to rush away to keep her appointment. Glancing at her watch, she realised with growing alarm that there was no way she was going to make it to the interview on time.

Perhaps it had been a mistake to walk to school. It had taken a lot longer than she'd anticipated, with Charlie dawdling and Becky stopping to search for wild flowers in the hedgerows, but this was a small island and she'd hoped she might get away without buying a car. Walking, she'd reasoned, would at least give them the opportunity to enjoy the green hills and valleys along the way and let them take in the view of the bay and the bustling harbour in the distance. Now, though, she still had a further ten minutes' walk ahead of her.

The hospital, she discovered, was relatively small, a pleasing, white-painted building, with a deep, low-slung roof. Alongside it was a health centre and a pharmacy. She hurried through the automated glass doors at the entrance.

The receptionist was talking to a young woman, a slender girl with chestnut hair arranged into an attractive braid at the back of her head. She was a doctor, Saskia guessed, judging by the stethoscope draped around her neck.

'Hello. Can I help you?' The receptionist broke off their conversation so that she could attend to the new arrival.

'Oh, hello. Yes, thanks,' Saskia said, a little out of breath from her exertions. 'I'm Dr Reynolds. I'm here to see Dr Gregson.'

'Oh, yes,' the woman answered with a smile, ticking her name off a list on her desk, 'you're the nine-fifteen appointment. They're waiting for you. If you'd like to come with me, I'll take you along to the office.'

The woman doctor glanced down at her watch and made a face. Noting her reaction,

Saskia almost did the same. She could guess what she was thinking. She wasn't making a very good start.

'Just tell Dr Beckett that I'd appreciate his involvement in the new cardiovascular clinic, would you?' the doctor murmured. 'Perhaps he might be able to spare me a few minutes later today?'

'I'm sure he'll make the time,' the receptionist answered.

She walked with Saskia along the corridor. 'Here we are,' she said, knocking lightly on a door marked in bold, black lettering 'Dr James Gregson'.

A gravelly voice responded, 'Come,' and Saskia pulled in a deep breath before going into the room. She took in her surroundings in one vague sweep.

A large, mahogany desk dominated the room, and behind it sat a well-dressed, distinguished-looking man who studied her with interest over rimless reading glasses that sat low down on his nose. There were two other, younger, men on either side of him, some small distance away, seated at an angle to the table.

One of them had his head down, immersed in studying papers in a manila file, and for a dreadful moment, as she stared at the top of his dark head, Saskia felt a wash of stomach-lurching familiarity run through her. Her heart began to thump, increasing in tempo as though she'd been running. Could this really be her new neighbour?

'Dr Reynolds, it's good to see you. Please, come in and take a seat.' Dr Gregson stood up and waved her to a leather chair in front of the desk. He was a man of medium build, with square-cut features and dark hair, greying a little at the temples. Above the glasses his brown eyes were keen, missing nothing.

'Let me introduce you to my colleagues,' he said. 'This is Dr Matheson—Noah Matheson. He's our man in charge of the minor injuries unit.'

Dr Matheson stood up to shake hands with her. He was young, handsome, in his early thirties, tall, lithe, and it was obvious right away that he was most definitely taken with Saskia. Interest sparked in his hazel eyes as he drank in the cloud of her Titian hair and his gaze skimmed her slender, curvaceous figure. She was wearing a cream-coloured suit with a pencil-line skirt and a jacket that nipped in at the waist. It was a feminine outfit yet at the same time business-like, and it gave her a fair amount of confidence to know that she looked her best.

'It's a pleasure to meet you,' Noah said, holding onto her hand for a second or two longer than was strictly necessary.

'And this is Dr Beckett—Tyler Beckett. He's in charge of Accident and Emergency.'

Her spirits plummeted, her worst fears confirmed.

Tyler stood up and clasped her hand firmly in his. His glance moved over her, clearly appreciative. His smile was warm, welcoming, and she relaxed a little. Maybe this wasn't going to be so bad after all. He looked terrific, lean and flat-stomached, every bit as good as the first day she'd seen him. The jacket of his suit was open, revealing a deep blue shirt teamed with a silver-grey tie. His cufflinks were of the same silver-grey pattern.

'Dr Reynolds and I have already met,' he said, addressing his colleagues. 'It turns out that she's a neighbour of mine.' He looked into her green eyes, adding in a low voice, 'I didn't know the name of our applicant until this morning, and even then I wasn't sure it would turn out to be you.' His well-shaped mouth made a faint curve. 'Perhaps I should have guessed as time went on. It sort of fitted somehow.' He didn't look at his watch, but she caught his drift all the same.

He released her and she sat down carefully. She cleared her throat. 'I must apologise for being so late,' she said, looking from one to another. How much should she tell them? 'I had a few unavoidable domestic issues to contend with this morning—and then the dog was sick just as I was leaving the house. Um…on top of that, I didn't realise quite how long it would take me to walk to the hospital.' She winced inwardly. She was babbling, wasn't she, saying too much? They didn't need to know all that. 'It was my mistake, but I'll be certain to make better arrangements from now on.'

'I'm sure you will.' Dr Gregson picked up a folder and leafed through it, saying after a while, 'Would you like to tell us a bit about your last post? You worked at a hospital in Cornwall, I believe?'

'That's right.' She was on much safer ground with this. 'I started off there as a senior house officer in the A and E department. I had to deal with all kinds of emergencies, both traumatic and general. A good percentage of my patients were youngsters.'

'That's valuable experience. Good...good...' Dr Gregson riffled through his papers. 'Your references are all in order from what I can see, and your qualifications are impeccable. You've specialised in emergency medicine and paediatrics, as well as spending some time in general practice—that's excellent, exactly what we're

looking for.' He glanced at her. 'It's a little unusual, though, to mix hospital work with general practice, isn't it?'

She faltered briefly, caught on the back foot.
'Ah…that's true, of course…but…initially I
wasn't sure which specialty appealed to me
the most.' She squirmed a little. Tyler Beckett would never be unsure of himself, would
he? 'I enjoyed working in a GP's surgery for
a year, but after attending several emergency
cases during that time I realised that's what I
wanted to do more than anything.'

Dr Gregson nodded. 'I see.' He turned to his
colleagues. 'Do you have any questions you'd
like to put to Dr Reynolds?'

Tyler nodded. 'I do have one query,' he said,
his tone sober. 'Ah…about these references…'
He was sifting through his copy of the paperwork, and she glanced at him, sitting stiffly
upright, suddenly on alert.

'Is there a problem?'

'Not a problem as such… I'm just a little

concerned about one aspect of your work that hasn't been mentioned here...'

She frowned. 'I can't think of anything I might have left out.'

He gave her a direct look. 'No, except—there was an occasion when you lost a patient, I believe. Would you like to tell us about that incident...about what happened?'

Saskia sucked in a sharp breath. 'But how did you...? I thought—' She broke off, uncertain where this line of questioning was coming from.

Noah frowned, sending Tyler a questioning, disbelieving look, as though he couldn't fathom why his colleague would want to upturn the apple cart this way.

'It's just something your previous consultant mentioned.' Tyler used a soothing voice, as though he wanted to put her at ease. 'I didn't fully understand the implications and I thought you might be able to clear it up for us.'

'M-my consultant?' She gazed at him in consternation, her green eyes troubled.

'Yes. It just happened that I rang the hospital in Truro this morning,' he explained, 'to enquire about a patient of mine who was recently admitted, and I was put on to Michael Drew. He was your consultant, wasn't he?'

Michael. The breath left her body in a soft gasp and her stomach began to churn. She might have known this would come up to bite her. She'd made a mistake, getting involved with Michael. In the end he'd been more than just her consultant, and that's when things had started to go downhill, hadn't they?

It had been fine at first. They'd dated for a time, and she'd enjoyed his company, but eventually, when she'd realised he was becoming too controlling, she'd called a halt to things between them. Michael hadn't taken it well, and eventually the situation between them had deteriorated to a point where life at work had become intolerable. That was partly why she'd made up her mind it was time to look around for another job.

And now this… It looked as though Michael

had thrown a spanner into the works at the worst possible time. She hadn't been able to avoid giving his name for a reference, and he'd assured her that she had nothing to worry about. But now—what could he have said to Tyler? Clearly their break-up still rankled with him, and although she'd hoped he would be adult about things, she really wouldn't put it past him to try to make life difficult for her.

Tyler watched the variety of expressions flit across her face. He said quietly, 'When I realised who he was, that you and he had worked together, we got to chatting, and that's when he mentioned your patient. He only brought it up as a humorous anecdote.'

Her mouth made a wry twist at that and he paused momentarily. 'He said you'd lost her and there was a big hue and cry until she was found again. But by then she needed treatment for another condition.'

He rested his hands on top of the file, lacing his fingers together. 'It might have seemed slightly amusing afterwards, when the worry was over, but I'm sure you can see why this has to be cleared up, can't you? We need to be reassured that our patients are going to be in the best possible hands.'

'Yes, of course, I understand perfectly.' Saskia moistened her lips, unhappily aware that Noah and Dr Gregson had both straightened and were paying her close attention. 'The truth is I didn't find anything at all humorous about the situation at any time, when it was going on or afterwards. And I didn't lose her— not exactly.'

'So, what happened?'

'She was a woman in her sixties suffering from what appeared to be dementia. A passerby had brought her into the hospital because she'd had a fall and hurt her arm.'

She was silent for a moment, remembering the hectic activity in the emergency unit that day. 'We were very busy in A and E that morning, and we were short-staffed. Some of the nurses were off sick with a bug that was going around. I didn't have anyone to assist me, but

I was keen to do further tests on my patient—alongside my concerns over her arm I wasn't absolutely convinced she had dementia. Anyway, I asked her to stay in the treatment cubicle while I went to find a porter to take the blood samples over to Pathology. But when I came back to see her a couple of minutes later, she'd gone walkabout.'

'That was tough luck,' Noah sympathised.

She nodded. 'It was worrying. We couldn't find her anywhere nearby. Then it occurred to me that she might have wandered outside into the hospital grounds so I followed the stairs to the exit. I found her sitting on the bottom step, nursing a swollen ankle. Apparently she'd missed her footing.'

Tyler's mouth made a wry shape. 'It just wasn't her day, was it?'

'No, unfortunately, it wasn't.'

'So, what was the final diagnosis?' he asked. His expression was thoughtful, his blue gaze skimming her features as though he was trying to weigh her up.

'She had a thyroid problem—her body was producing too little of the hormone, causing symptoms that mimicked dementia. And to add to her troubles she had a cracked bone in her forearm from the earlier fall, along with a sprained ankle from taking the stairs.'

Dr Gregson gave her a reassuring smile. 'Well, I think you've cleared that up for us nicely, Dr Reynolds. Thank you for that.' He looked at her over his glasses. 'And it's good to know that you weren't prepared to accept things at face value.'

She inclined her head briefly and tried to breathe slowly and steadily. That had been a deeply uncomfortable few moments. Tyler was clearly a stickler for getting things right, but she might have hoped he'd be less thorough in following up every detail arising from her application. Did he have to dot every i and cross every t? Michael could very easily have ruined things for her.

'You'll certainly need to be on the ball in this job,' Dr Gregson remarked. 'It isn't quite the same as being on the mainland where you have all manner of resources to hand. Those patients who are too ill to be managed in our small hospital have to be flown over to Cornwall for treatment.'

'I'm sure I'll be able to handle whatever's asked of me, Dr Gregson. I've had to cope with a huge change of circumstances recently but I think I'm dealing with it.'

Noah was clearly interested in this. 'Do you want to tell us more about that?'

She closed her eyes fleetingly, wishing she could take back the words and steeling herself against the pain. 'My brother and his wife were involved in a nasty road accident.' She took a deep breath. 'They're both in hospital in Truro at the moment—and it's beginning to look as though they'll be there for some time.'

Tyler frowned, leaning forward in his seat. 'You didn't mention this to me before, at the house.'

'No—perhaps I should have, but it was painful for me to talk about it. I was still getting over the shock. I still am.' She hesitated, then went on, 'They were preparing to move over here for Sam's job—he works for the wildlife trust and they wanted him as part of their team in the Isles of Scilly. Sam was bringing his family over that day so that they could see the house—they were going to rent before they decided where to make a permanent home. They wanted to spend some time looking around the island, but before they could get here they were in collision with a lorry that took a bend too wide. Luckily, the children escaped relatively unhurt, though they were traumatised, of course.'

'I'm sorry.' Tyler was genuinely concerned. 'That must have been devastating for you. And I suppose you've taken over caring for the children in the meantime?'

'That's right. That's why I came over here, and it's the reason I'm looking for work.'

'Is there no one else who can care for them?' Noah was full of compassion and understanding, although at the same time it seemed he sensed there was an opportunity to be explored here. 'Is there no one to support you—you've no ties?'

Tyler sent him a sharp look and Noah checked himself, drawing back.

Saskia shook her head. 'Not right now...at least, not close by.' She guessed Noah was never one to let the grass grow under his feet. With his looks and easygoing manner he'd probably left behind a string of female conquests who'd fallen for his charms.

'I admire your sense of loyalty,' Tyler said, frowning as he glanced through the paperwork once more, 'and I can see why finding work here must be important to you...but hadn't you handed in your notice before your brother's accident?'

Saskia's shoulders lifted awkwardly. Didn't he ever miss anything? 'I'd already decided I wanted a change.'

'Wasn't that a little irresponsible—to leave your job on a whim?'

She flattened her lips briefly. She wasn't

about to go into detail about her failed relationship. 'Perhaps it was,' she conceded, 'but the way I saw it there's pretty much always a need for emergency doctors in the UK.'

He nodded. 'On the mainland, maybe. I think you'll find there's not quite the same demand out here, though.'

'Yes, I'm starting to realise that.' Her heart sank. This wasn't going at all the way she'd hoped. From the doubts he was expressing it looked very much as though he didn't want her for this job, and she could hardly blame him.

For someone as thorough and organised as Tyler Beckett it would go against the grain to take on a young woman who appeared to work on impulse and followed wherever her heart led.

She didn't know how many people they had interviewed for this post, but she guessed she wasn't the only candidate. There had been at least three names on the receptionist's tick sheet.

'I did have another job in mind in Cornwall

at the time,' she ventured, 'and I was about to be interviewed for it, but all my plans had to change after the accident.'

Dr Gregson decided it was time to intervene. 'With regard to the post you're applying for here, you should understand that our work isn't just centred on the hospital. We often travel to the islands to visit patients in emergency situations. In those circumstances, we use the ambulance boat to reach them.'

'Oh, I see.' She swallowed carefully. She'd said she'd be able to cope with the demands of the job, but going by boat wasn't something she had bargained for. And yet it should have been fairly obvious to her that travelling between the islands was a necessity. Perhaps she'd simply tried not to think about it.

The trouble was, ever since she was a child she'd been plagued by seasickness—how could she possibly tell them that? If she owned up, there was absolutely no way she'd get the job.

'Does that bother you?' Tyler was watching

her, a small frown indenting his brow. 'You seem distracted somehow.'

She tried what she hoped was a convincing smile. 'No, not at all. I'd be quite all right with that.'

Dr Gregson appeared satisfied. 'Well, then, Dr Reynolds, my colleagues and I have one more person to interview before we get together to talk things through. We should be able to let you know our decision before the end of the morning, though. In the meantime, perhaps you'd like to look around our hospital— Janine, my secretary, will be happy to give you the grand tour. You might want to spend some time in the minor injuries unit to see how we do things there, and then familiarise yourself with the A and E department.'

She nodded. 'Yes, thank you. I would. That's a good idea.' At least she could stay around until they were ready to announce their decision.

His secretary showed her around the different areas of the hospital, pointing out the new

cardiovascular wing and the obstetrics department. They made light conversation along the
way, but Saskia felt weighed down inside with
defeat. In her imaginings things would have
gone very differently.

'We have a few inpatient beds here,' Janine
told her, 'but we're probably not at all like the
hospitals you've been used to. Everything here
is on a much smaller scale.'

Saskia nodded. 'I've been impressed with
what I've seen so far. It's all exceptionally clean
and efficient-looking.'

Finally, they arrived at the A and E department. There were a couple of resuscitation
rooms, several treatment bays and an area
where doctors could go to type up their notes
or access computers.

'I love the way this small area has been set
apart for the younger patients,' Saskia commented. 'That mural must help to take their
minds off their troubles, for a start.'

Janine smiled. 'It's great, isn't it? Dr Beckett
commissioned it from a relative of one of his

patients. The children love trying to find the chicks hiding in the farmyard. And, of course, the ceiling mural helps distract them when they have to lie down.'

'Yes, I imagine it does.' It had been made to look like a vivid blue sky, with cotton-wool clouds, a mixed assembly of birds and colourful box kites to keep the children amused.

If only she could be so easily distracted. She sighed inwardly, thinking about the members of the interview panel who were most likely deciding her fate at that very moment. Her stomach gave an uncomfortable lurch.

A nurse came over to them as they walked towards the nurses' station. 'Janine, I've been paging Dr Beckett—do you know if he's in the hospital today? I haven't seen him all morning and we've had a patient come in with an injury to his wrist. We need him to come and take a look at it.'

'He's definitely here. He's been doing interviews since first thing, but they should be finished by now. I expect he'll be along in a minute or two.'

'Okay, thanks.'

Janine glanced at Saskia. 'You might want to be in on this—see how we do things here.'

'Are you sure?' Saskia frowned. 'I don't want to get in the way.'

Janine shook her head. 'I'm sure it won't be a problem. We're all very friendly and informal around here.'

'You have a patient for me?' Dr Beckett strode into the A and E unit, his manner brisk and ready for action. Saskia stiffened. Had the interview panel finished their discussion and come to a conclusion?

'He's in here,' the triage nurse told him, pointing out one of the treatment rooms. 'We've done X-rays and given him painkillers.' She handed him the patient's file.

'Thanks.' He glanced at the notes in the file, and then went over to the computer and studied the films. Frowning, he said, 'I'll need someone to assist. Who's free?'

The nurse shook her head. 'No one right now. I'm needed in several places at once, and as for the rest—we're busy with an influx of patients just now. There was a minor explosion at a building site and we've had a number of casualties…something to do with a propane gas cylinder. Nothing dreadfully serious regarding casualties, thankfully, but some quite nasty burns.'

He inclined his head in acknowledgement. 'Okay, I suppose I'll just have to wait until you can spare someone.'

Saskia said quickly, 'I could help, if you want.'

He glanced at her. 'Are you sure?'

'Of course. If there's anything at all I can do…' She frowned. 'I understand this man has a broken wrist. Was that something to do with the explosion?'

He shook his head. 'Totally different, apparently. He came off his motorcycle while taking a bend too sharply.'

'Oh, dear.'

They went into the treatment room, where they found a young man in his early twenties nursing a badly deformed wrist.

'Well, Mason,' Tyler said, pulling up a chair and carefully examining the man's injury, 'I could have told you even without looking at the X-rays that you've broken your wrist.' He glanced at Saskia. 'Have you seen this kind of fracture before?'

She nodded. 'It's a Smith's fracture,' she murmured, 'and that's a typical garden-spade deformity.' She looked at Mason. 'I expect you fell awkwardly off your bike and landed on the back of your hand. I suppose you can count yourself lucky you don't have any other injuries—apart from cuts and grazes, that is.'

The young man gave her a rueful smile. 'I guess I can. Though this feels bad enough.'

'I'm sure it does.'

'We'll get you sorted out in no time,' Tyler said. 'I'll give you a local anaesthetic and a sedative, and then we'll realign the bones for you and get you fixed up with a splint.' He looked at

Saskia. 'I'll need you to hold his elbow steady while I reduce the fracture—are you okay with that?'

'Yes, of course.'

A few minutes later, when their patient's wrist had been fully anaesthetised, they worked together to manipulate the bones back into position. 'Okay,' Tyler said, checking the shape of the wrist and testing the pulses there. 'That seems to have done the trick. We'll get that splinted up and then do further X-rays to make sure everything's as it should be.'

Mason was clearly relieved some time later when the procedure was finished and had been pronounced a success.

'Okay, we'll see you back here in a couple of days to check how things are going,' Tyler told him. 'And in the meantime I'll write up a prescription for some painkillers for you to take home with you.'

'Thanks.'

At Tyler's signal, a nurse came to take Mason along to the nurses' station so that she could go through the discharge process with him and give him his medication.

Tyler turned to Saskia. 'Thanks for your help with that. I'm sure he was relieved to get it over and done with.' His glance moved over her fleetingly. 'You've been very patient. You must be anxious to know the result of your interview?'

She nodded. 'Has it been decided?'

He shook his head. 'Not yet. I gave the others my input before I left the meeting, so I expect they'll let us know shortly. Shall we go along to my office while we wait? I expect you could do with a cup of coffee.'

'That would be good, thanks,' she said, although all she really wanted to do now was get out of there and start working out what she was going to do for the best. She didn't hold out much hope for a successful outcome.

His office was everything she might have expected. It was a beautifully turned out room with satisfying neutral colours in soft greys and blues and an overall sense of calm. A good deal of light came in through deep, wide windows that looked out onto a paved terrace beyond, where stone planters were filled with bright chrysanthemums, adding a splash of colour.

The furniture was made of pale golden beechwood. A desk with a pigeonholed upstand stood to one side of the room, and against another wall neat cupboards were interspersed with glass-fronted bookcases. There were even a couple of plants, billowy ferns that provided a pleasing touch of green.

'Please, sit down,' he said, waving her towards a chair. He switched on the filter machine, and soon the delicious aroma of coffee filled the room.

'I'm sorry if I seemed a bit hard on you this morning,' he said, placing a cup on the desk beside her. 'I know it must have been difficult for you.'

She took a sip of the hot liquid. 'I had the feeling you weren't at all keen on having me as part of your team,' she murmured, 'though I don't really know what you have against me.'

'It's not that I don't want you,' he demurred. He went to stand with his back to the window. 'I have one or two reservations, that's all. I have the feeling that you're inclined to be impulsive—which is not a bad thing at all unless it intrudes on your work, but it wouldn't do to be making impulsive decisions in A and E.'

'Unless they were based on instinctive knowledge, maybe.'

He shrugged. 'Possibly. The other thing is that I can't help feeling you're holding something back. I'm not sure yet what that might be.'

He studied her once more, but she didn't offer any explanation. Instead, she lowered her head and swallowed her coffee as though it was a lifesaver.

He appeared to be deep in thought for a while, but then he said, 'I suppose the biggest hurdle for me was that I had a particular type of candidate in mind—someone who was on the ball, alert and ready to face up to the challenges of the job.'

He smiled, gentle humour reflected in his eyes and in the curve of his mouth. 'But instead you came along—and from what I saw back at the house you strike me as being... distracted, disorganised and probably stressed out with the strain of looking after your family. Medicine's a difficult profession, even for the hardiest of people, and I can't help feeling that this is probably not the best time for you to be taking on a responsible position.'

Dismayed, she stared at him. 'You can't judge me on one meeting. You must realise that you came to the house at a particularly difficult time.'

'Yes...but that one time made a big impression on me.' He made a wry face. 'The problem is I'm finding it difficult to be detached when it comes to making this decision. Try as I may to keep a clear mind, the fact is whenever I look at you, in my mind's eye I keep seeing a beautiful, half-naked young woman surrounded by chaos. It's kind of hard to shake off that image.'

Her cheeks flushed with hot colour. 'I... You

caught me unawares. I wasn't ready to receive visitors.'

He chuckled. 'No, I realised that, and I should have left right away, but I must admit, the temptation to stay was just too great.'

She sucked in a sharp breath. 'Tyler, I need this job.'

He nodded. 'I know,' he said, becoming serious once more. 'And the truth is we need a woman on the team to balance things up. I might be a bit concerned that you're not exactly what I had in mind, but I suppose, since we would be working together initially, I'd be able to keep an eye on you.'

Her eyes widened. 'Are you saying that you voted in my favour?'

'I am, albeit with reservations.' The phone rang just then and he came over to the desk to half sit, half lean on the edge as he reached for the receiver. She was conscious of him being close to her, the fabric of his trousers stretched taut against his thigh, and she felt a sudden, unbidden, rush of heat race through her veins.

'Okay, thanks,' he said to whoever was on the other end of the line. 'Will do.'

He replaced the receiver and looked at her. 'That was Dr Gregson. He said to tell you the job's yours if you want it.'

She gave a small gasp. 'Really? Oh, I do. Definitely, I do.'

His mouth curved, giving his features an irresistible sex appeal. 'Good. That's settled, then.' His expression sobered. 'Though there is one proviso I should add.'

'And that is…?' She frowned, on edge all over again.

'We feel there should be a three-month trial period to give us all time to decide whether we think things will work out. It'll be a mutual arrangement. After all, you may decide you don't care for the way we do things here, and once your brother and his wife are out of hospital, you may want to go back to the mainland.'

She mulled it over. Right now, she couldn't see that happening, because she would always want to be close to her family, but it was true she had friends back in Cornwall, people she would miss.

'I can see how a three-month trial might work both ways.' She was troubled, though. This result was a positive one for the time being, but it wasn't quite what she'd hoped for, not with this inevitable sense of insecurity hanging over her. Tyler was the one who would have pushed for that condition, she was sure. How could she convince him that she wouldn't let him down?

She said carefully, 'Look, I know you have your doubts about me, but I'm sure I can show you that I'm as sensible and methodical as you or anyone else.'

She thought about it for a moment or two and then added hastily, 'In fact, why don't you come over for supper one evening…Saturday, perhaps? Then I can show you that I don't always live surrounded by chaos and upheaval. You'll see, I can be every bit as efficient and on the ball as you are.'

'You don't have to do that—'

'I know. I want to.'

He inclined his head a fraction. 'Then, yes, thank you. I'd like that—that is, provided I'm not called out to any sudden emergencies.' He frowned. 'I believe I'm on call over the weekend. I wouldn't want to put you to any trouble unnecessarily.'

'Don't worry about that. I always cook too much, anyway. I haven't managed to work out everyone's appetites yet. But if you can make it, that would be good. I'll look forward to it.' She hesitated. 'Um—do you have any particular likes or dislikes about food? I mean, I'd hate to come up with something hot and spicy, for instance, if you couldn't abide that kind of thing.'

'I like hot and spicy, and I'm willing to try anything,' he said. 'But please don't go to a lot of bother. I know you have enough to cope with already.'

'I'll be fine,' she answered with as much confidence as she could muster, but her smile was strained as she left his office a few minutes later. What was she doing, acting as though she was so self-assured? How on earth did she know that she could carry it off? Life was anything but routine for her these days and heaven alone knew what she was letting herself in for.

CHAPTER THREE

'YOU MADE IT, then—there were no callouts to drag you away, after all.' Saskia did her best to put on a cheerful front as she opened the door to her neighbour and soon-to-be boss. Everything had to go well today. She mentally crossed her fingers, smiling at Tyler as she stood to one side to let him into the house.

'Not one,' he agreed, stepping into the hallway and handing her a bottle of chilled wine. 'I hope this is all right. I thought it might go down well with supper and it would help us to celebrate your new job.'

'Thanks. That was thoughtful of you.'

'It was the least I could do, to make some small contribution.' He smiled, a faint curve to his mouth that had the unexpected effect of making her go weak at the knees, so that she had to inwardly shake herself to pull herself together. He was her boss—she had to keep remembering that. She wasn't going to even think about him any other way. She'd been down that road before, and look where it had led her.

It didn't help, though, that he looked fantastic. His appearance was flawless as usual, with black chinos moulding his long, muscled legs and a deep blue, open-necked shirt resting easily against the smooth, flat line of his stomach. It was very unsettling.

'Actually, I wasn't sure whether you would still be up for it,' he murmured. 'Supper, I mean. I noticed you've been out for most of the day. I saw you all leave early this morning, and I knew when you'd come back because I heard the children.' He looked concerned. 'I can't help thinking this must all have been a bit of a rush for you.'

'Uh…yes, it has been a bit hectic, but it's okay.' She frowned, thinking about the trip they'd made to Cornwall, and a shiver of unhappiness snaked down her spine. 'We went to visit my brother and his wife in hospital on the mainland.'

She led the way to the kitchen and placed the bottle of wine in the fridge before turning to look at him once more. 'It was a bit of a last-minute, spur-of-the-moment decision. The children have been desperate to go and see their parents, but neither Sam nor Megan has been well enough to receive visitors up to now. Then, when I phoned the hospital this morning, the nurse said they might be able to cope with a brief visit and I thought maybe we should make the trip over there.'

She flicked the switch on the coffee filter machine and waved him to a chair.

'It sounds as though they were involved in a really bad accident,' he commented, frowning as he sat down by the pale oak table. 'What exactly happened to them? Do you mind talking about it?'

She shook her head. 'No, it's all right. I think I'm over the worst now. It was just such a shock before.' She set out cups, a sugar bowl, and filled a small jug with cream. 'Sam had a really bad chest injury—they had to open up his chest to give him heart massage. Megan's was a blunt abdominal trauma, with a pelvic fracture.' Just thinking about it gave her chills.

He sucked in his breath. 'That must have been horrendous. It sounds as though they're lucky to be alive.'

'Yes, it was touch and go for both of them.' She slid a cup of coffee towards him and took a sip of hers to soothe her nerves. 'It was a relief to be able to see them today.'

'I'm sure it was,' he agreed, 'and I dare say it was good for them to see the children, too.'

'Yes, I think it cheered them up a bit. It's not easy for any of them, with the family being split up like this.'

He nodded. 'It's bound to be difficult.' He frowned, pausing momentarily before saying in a cautious tone, 'Was everything all right when you arrived back home? Only I couldn't help hearing a lot of shouting. Were the children upset by the visit?'

'Oh…' It was disturbing that he was so aware of everything that was going on in her life. 'Um…they were all a bit unsettled, but I suppose that was to be expected. Charlie, especially, was shocked to see his mum and dad looking so ill.' She pulled a face. 'But I think the shouting was over something different. That was because of Boomer.'

'Oh?' He gave a wry smile. 'More trouble?'

'Oh, yes.' She grimaced, remembering the havoc that had greeted her on their arrival home. 'I think he objected to being cooped up on his own for so long. He'd taken out his frustration on the rug in the living room—we found it in bits all over the floor.' She saw his frown and said quickly, 'I'll pay for a replacement, of course.' As the landlord, he must be wondering just how much damage this family could inflict on his property.

She hurried on. 'Not content with that, he'd sunk his teeth into Caitlin's electronic photo album and Charlie's steering-wheel—you know, those things they use with computer games? Then Caitlin had a set-to with Charlie over him rummaging through things in her room, and Charlie started arguing with Becky over tidying up his toys so well that he couldn't find something he wanted.' She shrugged awkwardly. 'Things blew up out of proportion. I think it was probably something to do with the aftermath of the visit—they were all a bit strung out. So everything escalated and it was as though all hell was let loose in here for a while.'

He seemed perplexed by the sheer chaos she described. 'I'd no idea family life could be so fraught. I'm much more used to an orderly way of going on. I'm not sure I could deal with what you're having to put up with of late.'

He finished off his coffee and said briskly, 'But that was bad luck with the dog—don't worry about the rug. Hopefully, it was a one-off and we can mark it down to experience.' He was thoughtful for a moment and then asked on a reflective note, 'Isn't it going to be a problem for you when you start work? I mean, Boomer's not going to take kindly to being left at home, from the sound of things. That could prove to be something of a problem.'

She winced inwardly. She might have known he would pick up on that. 'Yes, that's true, and I've been giving it some thought.' She pulled in a deep breath. 'I've arranged for someone to come in and walk him a couple of times a day. She's the wife of someone who knows my brother, Sam, through his work, so I know she's trustworthy and I'm pretty sure she'll be dependable. She likes dogs and offered to help when she heard I'd be going out to work. She even said she'd lend a hand with the children if ever I was stuck, so she's a good friend to have.'

'It certainly looks that way.' He glanced at Boomer, who was sleeping in a corner of the room, worn out after his rampage, and said with a faint smile, 'It's a shame she wasn't around earlier today.'

'Yes. Unfortunately, when I made the phone call I made up my mind to go there and then and I didn't think too much about what would happen while we were out.' She frowned. She'd been far too busy making arrangements for them to get to the ferry on time and trying to work out how she would fit in all the preparations for supper once they got home. She'd only just remembered in time to take her travel sickness pills.

Of all the days for Boomer to decide to create havoc, this was one of the worst. Five hours there and back on the ferry hadn't done much to help anybody's temper and her stress level had been rising steadily since they'd arrived back.

Still, she wasn't doing too badly. She'd found time to shower and change into a little black dress that clung to her in all the right places and that at least helped to boost her confidence. She'd seen Tyler's glance skim her figure more than once since he'd arrived, so perhaps it was having the desired effect. Things might not be so bad after all.

As for supper, she'd chosen a Mexican theme—it was a favourite with the children and she hoped Tyler would like it, too.

The enchiladas, filled with tender chicken and vegetables then topped with sauce and a generous coating of grated cheese, were baking in the oven—a quick fifteen minutes was all that was needed to melt the cheese—and the rice was steaming gently on the hob. She went over there now and lifted the lid on the pan so that she could peer inside.

Tyler sniffed the air appreciatively. 'Something smells good.'

'Oh, thanks. I thought I'd go for something spicy...chicken enchiladas and Mexican rice.' A sudden qualm hit her. 'Would that be okay for you? I mean, if not I could—'

'That sounds absolutely fine,' he said quickly, and she tried to relax a little.

'Oh, good. I've made some dips to go along with it, and I have some cheesecake for dessert.' She was an idiot. What would she have done if he'd said no—started again with something simple, like cheese on toast? She was far too jumpy. She must calm down.

'It should be ready any time now.' So far, despite her anxieties, everything was going according to plan. She even allowed herself a quiet moment of satisfaction but that small oasis of peace was brutally shattered when, all of a sudden, shrill voices erupted from the living room and spilled over into the kitchen. The smile froze on her lips. What now?

'I'm keeping it. I found it.' It was Charlie's voice.

'No, you didn't. You stole it. It's mine. Saskia gave it to me.' Becky marched into the room, righteous indignation bringing hot colour to her cheeks as she glared furiously at her brother.

'What are you two arguing about?' Saskia threaded her fingers through her hair, trying to push back her unruly curls. It was hot in the kitchen, and she was overly conscious of anything that threatened to disrupt her timetable.

A ripple of alarm ran through her at this latest intrusion. Everything had to run smoothly if she was to make a good impression on Tyler— she needed to finish setting the table, add a squeeze of lime juice to the salsa, stir cheese into the rice, and take the enchiladas from the oven. What else was there to do? Her mind had suddenly gone blank.

'He's got my buzzy bee pencil,' Becky complained, stormclouds brewing in her eyes.

'It was on the floor, so now it's mine,' Charlie retorted. 'If I hadn't picked it up, Boomer would have had it.'

'That doesn't count. It's mine. Give it back.' Becky gave him a push.

Charlie shoved back hard in return and Becky's flailing arms sent a potted plant flying through the air like a guided missile. It landed on the floor, breaking into a mess of shattered china, soil and broken fronds.

Through all this, Saskia was ultra-conscious of Tyler, who had sprung to his feet to steady Becky and was now standing by the worktop, watching everything with an air of bemused expectation.

She braced herself. 'Enough,' she said. 'All this fuss is about a pencil?' She couldn't believe this was happening to ruin her careful preparations. What would he think of them, and of her ability to cope? 'Where is it? Let me see.' She held out a hand, and Charlie reluctantly passed it to her.

'Well, if it's going to cause all this fuss, perhaps no one should have it—for now, at any rate.' She put it away in a cupboard, high up where neither of them could reach.

'That's not fair!'

'Give it back!'

'You can have it back after supper, Becky. For now, why don't both of you go and see if you can fill in some more pieces to the jigsaw puzzle? You like doing that.'

Both children were scowling at her now, and she said quietly, 'Out of the kitchen now, both of you. I'm trying to cook here.' She felt as though she'd been parachuted into the middle of a menagerie.

She glanced at Tyler. 'I'm sorry about all the noise,' she said. 'I thought I'd settled them down with colouring books and word puzzles, but it looks as though their interest has worn thin. And Charlie's been out of sorts ever since we went over to the hospital.'

'It looks that way, doesn't it?' He seemed distracted, then added in a vaguely warning tone, 'You know, I don't want to tell you your business, but I think I can smell something burning.'

Saskia looked at him, her whole body stiffening. In all the confusion had she missed the alert of the kitchen timer? With every minute that passed she could see her well-laid plans turning to rubble all around her.

She gave a small gasp. 'The enchiladas…the rice.'

Becky and Charlie hadn't moved from the spot and now they were looking on, wide-eyed as she skirted the broken plant pot to turn off the heat under the pan of rice. Then with growing trepidation she reached into the oven to slide out the hot baking trays.

It was scary how fast things could fall apart. 'They're burnt,' Charlie pronounced in his usual blunt fashion, and her shoulders slumped a little.

'Um…I don't think they're too bad,' she said, a dubious note creeping into her voice.

Tyler glanced at the once perfect tortilla wraps. 'Actually, I think it's only the edges that are a little overdone,' he murmured, 'just where the sauce has stuck a bit. Shall I ease them out for you? Do you have a spatula?'

'Uh…yes, I'll get it for you. Thanks.'

She handed him the spatula and fetched the serving trays from the warming oven. It was bad enough that he'd been here to witness all the shouting that had been going on, but now…what must he think of her? He probably thought that if she couldn't handle things in the kitchen, she would be hopeless in the emergency room—but it wasn't true, that was totally different. She was good at her job and she could handle A and E as though she had been born to it...even though Michael had made life difficult for her and tried to undermine her and trip her up at every opportunity after their split.

Swiftly, she pulled herself together. 'Charlie, go and fetch the dustpan and brush, please, and sweep up that plant. Becky, we need the guacamole and salsa to be put out on the table, and then perhaps you could go and tell Caitlin that supper's ready.'

What had possessed her to invite Tyler here? How could he ever see her at her best in these circumstances? She wasn't used to having children around. In her normal, everyday life she was organised, capable, efficient. Wasn't she... most of the time?

She sagged against the cupboard, wiping her forehead with the back of her hand, and gazed for a moment into space, gathering her wits.

'How about a glass of wine?' Tyler popped the cork on the bottle he had brought with him and hunted for glasses in the cupboards. 'That might make you feel a bit better.'

She managed a smile. 'Thanks. That's a good idea.'

She swallowed the smooth, chilled wine gratefully, and then put down her glass and set to work to serve up the meal. Tyler found dinner plates warming in the oven and put them out on the table, along with a jug of orange juice for the children. Between them, they set out platters of enchiladas and tortilla chips along with a dish of hot Mexican rice and a salad bowl that she'd prepared earlier.

'It doesn't look bad at all,' Tyler commented charitably, and Saskia winced.

'Caitlin says she doesn't want anything to eat.' Becky came and sat down at the table, surveying all the food on display. 'I'm starving,' she said.

Saskia frowned. Caitlin wasn't coming downstairs? Something was definitely not right with her. She'd not been herself for days now and she really needed to get to the root of what was wrong.

'Are you worried about her?' Tyler asked, watching her expression. 'If you want to go up and have a chat with her, we'll be fine here.'

'Are you sure? I really feel I ought to...' She threw him an apologetic look. 'But, please, make a start on the food before it gets cold.'

'Don't worry about it. We'll be fine.' He looked at Becky and Charlie for agreement and they both nodded vigorously, pushing their plates forward slightly as he started to serve out the food.

Saskia hesitated, waiting as Charlie cut the singed ends from his enchilada and tentatively bit into it. He savoured it for a second or two, and then said, 'Yeah, that's good.'

Relieved, she hurried away to find Caitlin. It would be something of an achievement if she could persuade her to come down and try just a morsel of food, but she'd have to tread carefully. The teenager had been very touchy of late.

'I feel a bit sick,' Caitlin said. 'I just want to lie down for a bit.'

'Are you worrying about anything?' Saskia asked, sitting down on the bed beside her, but Caitlin gave a slight, negative shake of her head and didn't answer. 'Did it upset you, seeing your mum and dad today?'

'Yeah, it did a bit.' Caitlin bit her lip. 'They're really ill, aren't they? Mum looked as if she was in a lot of pain, and Dad was white as a sheet.'

'That's true, but they're in the right place,' Saskia said carefully. 'I had a word with the nurse, and she's going to ask the doctor to pre-scribe a different painkiller for your mother. They're both being well looked after and they should start to get better from now on.'

She talked to her niece for a while, gently stroking the girl's silky hair. 'Are you sure you won't come down and try some food—just a little?'

'I'm not hungry.'

'Okay. I'll save some for you in case you change your mind later on.'

She went to join the others in the kitchen and found the three of them talking animatedly about the latest game that Charlie was playing on his Xbox. 'The dragons breathe fire and you can cast spells on people,' Charlie was saying.

Tyler smiled. 'Wow, that sounds great.' He looked up as Saskia came into the room and said softly, 'How is she?'

'Worrying about her mum and dad, I think. It's been a difficult day for her...for us all.'

'I miss them,' Becky said, her eyes suddenly bright with unshed tears. 'They looked really poorly.'

Charlie stopped eating and looked at Saskia. 'When will they come home?' There was a wobble in his voice. 'I don't like them being so far away.'

'I know, sweetheart. I understand how you both feel.' She looked at the children, saddened by the distress she saw written on their faces. 'I'm not sure yet when they'll be home, but they're getting stronger every day, and that's good, isn't it? I know you miss them. It's hard, having to get used to what's happened, but we'll look after each other, and together we'll get through this the best way we can.'

They were still clearly upset, and Saskia searched for some way to steer them away from this downhill path.

'Perhaps you could make them a card or take them something that will cheer them up next time you visit?' Tyler suggested.

Becky nodded, while Charlie looked thought-ful. 'Like a box with sweets in it? Dad likes mints and toffees. I could make a box out of card…'

'That sounds like a good idea.' Tyler gave him an encouraging smile. 'Maybe you and Becky could make one each?'

'Yeah.' Becky's mind had ticked into craft mode. 'I want to make one for Mummy…one with shiny love hearts on it.' The children looked at one another and returned to their food with renewed vigour. They obviously wanted to get started on their project straight away.

Saskia sent Tyler a quick, grateful look. 'Thanks,' she said softly. 'That could have been difficult.'

'It's an awkward situation.'

They ate their meal, chatting about this and that. 'Are your parents able to help out while all this is going on?' Tyler asked after a while.

'My parents divorced some years ago,' she told him as she spooned more rice on to her plate. 'Now my father lives in Spain, and we don't really get to see him all that often. My mother eventually married again and moved to Somerset. She runs her own company so it's difficult for her to get away for long periods of time, but she's very worried about what's happening. She visits Sam as often as she's able to.' She glanced at him. 'What about you? Do you have any family close by?'

He nodded. 'My mother lives not too far away from here, and I have a younger sister who's working as an office manager in Tresco. I keep in touch with them on a regular basis. We've always been very close.'

She frowned. 'And your father?'

'He died a few years back—a heart attack.'

'Oh, I'm sorry. That must have been very difficult for you.'

'It was unexpected; it came out of the blue so, yes, it was painful at the time.'

She tried to imagine him with his mother and sister. He'd probably be very protective of them, especially of his sister, taking the place of the father they had lost.

They finished the main course, and he helped her to clear away the dishes. 'That was good,' he told her. 'Very tasty.'

'I suppose it wasn't too bad, once we'd rescued it from the inferno,' she said with a bleak smile. 'It's kind of you to say so, anyway.' She took the cheesecake from the fridge and placed it in the centre of the table. 'Perhaps this will make up for any failings in the first course.'

It did look good, a crumbly biscuit base, topped with cream cheese and generously covered with luscious strawberries. Charlie's eyes widened. 'Yum!'

'Definitely yum,' Tyler said with a grin, as they tucked in. He freshened Saskia's glass of wine and proposed a toast. 'Here's to your new job. Let's drink to it working out well.'

She clinked glasses with him, wondering if she would manage to convince him that she was the right person for the job. He seemed to be on her side, for the moment at least, so maybe things would work out all right after all.

Then again, a three-month trial might throw up all manner of pitfalls along the way. What if Tyler were to speak to Michael again? That could easily happen if he transferred patients over there—he'd already shown that he liked to check up on their progress to reassure himself that all was well.

Would Michael try to discredit her all over again? Maybe he couldn't do it professionally, but it wouldn't be beyond him to tell lies about her private life. He'd done that once before when she'd refused to take him back after their break-up. He'd hinted that she'd slept around and cheated on him, both outright lies. She'd been fortunate in that her friends knew she wasn't like that. They knew that she'd always behaved with honesty and integrity, but people who didn't know her so well might have har-boured doubts.

'Is something wrong?'

She looked up, startled out of her reverie by Tyler's gentle probing. How did he manage to read her so easily?

'No, nothing at all,' she said. 'I was just think-ing about what lies ahead. If you'd told me two months ago that I would up sticks and move to the Isles of Scilly to look after three children, a dog and a pet rabbit, I'd have said you were way out. And yet here I am.' She frowned.

'My life has changed so much lately. Instead of being footloose and fancy-free, I'm doing laundry for four, and most mornings I end up doing some last-minute ironing because there's something they've forgotten to tell me they need. And then there are school bags and gym kit to be found and lunch money that needs to be handed out.'

Charlie's ears pricked up at that. 'I need some money for Tuesday for swimming lessons. We're going on the bus. And I need some new swimming trunks.'

She gave him a puzzled look. 'Did I get a letter about this?'

He thought about it. 'Yeah.'

'I don't remember it. Where is it?'

He frowned. 'In my school bag.'

Saskia glanced at Tyler. 'I guess that's another job for the end of the school day—checking the school bags for scraps of paper.'

His mouth quirked at the corners. 'I'm sure you're doing the best you can.'

They finished dessert, and while Saskia started to make coffee Becky and Charlie shot off upstairs to rummage through their craft boxes.

'Thanks for inviting me here today,' Tyler said a few minutes later as he drank coffee, standing by the worktop. 'It's been...' he hesitated '…an experience. I have to admit I'm not used to the ups and downs of family life…not like this, anyway.'

'Me neither. I always got on well with my brother.'

'It was the same for me with my sister. I suppose I looked out for her. Still do, to a certain extent. Things at home were…complicated. But I like my life how it is now. I like the challenge of work in the emergency department, and I look forward to the contrast of peace and quiet when I get home.'

Saskia bit her lip. It had definitely been a mistake to invite him over here.

She glanced out of the window. Darkness was falling outside, filling the garden with inky-black shadows. 'I know things didn't go quite to plan this evening, but I'm glad you came. I thought it might be a good way for us to get to know one another—since we're neighbours and it looks as though we'll be working together quite closely.'

He nodded. 'It was a good idea.'

Her brow furrowed. 'Actually, I'm not sure exactly what that involves—working together, I mean.'

At the interview it had sounded as though he expected her to slip up at some point and he wanted to be there to prevent any mistakes from happening. 'I'm assuming we'll both be in A and E, dealing with our own patients, and I'll refer to you as the head of the team.'

'That's right. But initially we'll go out on call together, so that you'll get the lie of the land more easily. The same applies to going over to the hospital in Cornwall, should the need arise—at least until you find your feet.'

'Oh, I see. Well, that will certainly help.' He was being casual about it, but the truth remained that he would be keeping an eye on her. She'd have to earn his trust.

'In fact,' he said, 'I could give you a lift in to work every day, if you like. There's no point in us both going separately, is there?'

'No, that's true...' She was startled by his unexpected offer. 'That would be great...it's really thoughtful of you…but I have to take the children to school…'

'That's okay. We'll drop them off on the way.'

'That's very good of you. I appreciate it.'

He was being helpful, co-operative, and she could only hope she would live up to his expectations. Perhaps the situation with Michael had shaken her confidence and filled her with self-doubt. He'd made her question every action she'd taken, every drug she'd prescribed. Towards the end he'd made her life at work seem like hell on earth.

Troubled by these unsettling thoughts, she moved over to the sink unit, where Tyler was standing. She needed something to do to keep herself active and shake off the negativity of the past. It was dark outside now, an inky blackness, and she reached over to close the blind just as Tyler decided to set down his coffee cup on the draining board. Their bodies met in a soft collision. His hand lightly brushed the swell of her hip and an instant shock wave of heat pulsed through her body.

'Uh, I'm sorry.' He drew back as though he'd been stung.

'It's all right,' she managed, struggling to calm the pounding beat of her heart. 'It was an accident.'

'Yes.' He was watching her, seemingly mesmerised by her. His blue gaze drifted down over the gentle curves of her body, outlined by the soft material of the black dress. She could feel the warmth of his gaze searing her skin, almost as though he'd touched her, and her heart skipped a beat. A pulse began to throb at the base of her throat, an erratic, fluttery sensation that made her catch her breath.

Neither of them moved. It was as though they were imprisoned in some kind of force field where all her senses were heightened. He felt it too, she was sure.

Slowly, the magnetic tension that held them began to dissipate. In the background she could hear the thud of children's footsteps clattering down the stairs. The spell was broken and

Tyler glanced towards the kitchen door as the sound drew nearer.

'I—uh… Perhaps I should be going now,' he said huskily. 'It sounds as though you're going to be needed soon.' He drew in a quick breath. 'Thanks again for supper. I—uh—I must return the favour some time.'

'That's okay, you're welcome.' She managed to find her voice, even though her throat was suddenly bone dry. 'I'll see you out.'

He left by the back door, looking back briefly before setting off down the moonlit path at the side of the house. She acknowledged him with a wave.

After he'd gone, she stood for some time, slowly breathing in the night air, trying to get her thoughts back together.

He had an extraordinary effect on her, and it seemed that he wasn't immune to her either. That could be tricky. She wasn't looking for a relationship, didn't want to get involved with any man after her experience with Michael. She hadn't bargained for any of this when she'd come here, or when she'd applied for the job at the hospital.

But now it looked as though they might both be treading on dangerous ground, and if this evening's events were anything to go by, she'd have to be on her guard.

She was just getting over one bad experience, and she wasn't about to let herself in for another.

CHAPTER FOUR

'HEY, IT'S GOOD to see you, Saskia.' Noah Matheson caught up with Saskia and Tyler at the entrance to A and E. 'Are you all set for your first day with us?'

'I think so.' She returned his smile. 'Thanks for asking.'

'You'll do fine, I'm sure, but if you have any problems, just holler. I'll be right next door.' He waved a hand in the direction of the minor injuries unit.

'I'll remember that. Thanks. Though I'm hoping Tyler will be here to help me out, for the next few weeks at least.' She looked at Tyler and he inclined his head in acknowledgement.

Noah shot him a quick glance. 'Hmm… luck of the devil, that one.' He leaned closer to Saskia, saying in a stage whisper, 'Just remember, if you need anything at all, I'm your man.'

'Of course you are.' She laughed at his teasing. Noah was never going to be serious, was he? He was one of life's charmers, a cheerful, buoyant soul who couldn't resist trying his luck.

Tyler gave him a steely-eyed look. 'We'll see you later, Noah,' he said firmly. He rested a hand lightly in the small of Saskia's back and shepherded her away from their colleague and through the doors of the A and E unit.

Saskia was all too aware of Tyler's gentle but determined guidance. His touch was warm and supportive, sending ripples of heat eddying along her spine in a way that was profoundly unsettling. It flustered her, and she could only hope he wouldn't notice the flush of colour that swept along her cheekbones.

He was oblivious to the effect he was having on her, though, wasn't he? There wasn't anything to read into his innocent action. All Tyler wanted was to put some distance between her and Noah, because they both knew his colleague had the potential to be way too much of a distraction.

Once in the emergency department he was completely businesslike, introducing her to the staff on duty and showing her the areas she might have missed on her brief tour on the day of the interview.

'We keep lab request forms in here,' he told her, opening up a cupboard that housed myriad specialist documents, blank charts and so on. 'You'll find swabs, dressings, et cetera, in the cabinet over there, and tubing, surgical gloves and specimen bottles are stored in the cupboard right next to it.'

'Okay, I'll remember that.'

'It'll probably take a while for you to get to know where everything is, but the nurses are always willing to help out if you're unsure of anything.' His mouth made a crooked line. 'Most important place of all, of course, is the staff lounge. That's our main port of call for coffee, tea, biscuits and offloading all the frustrations of the day. It's along here.'

He led the way down a wide corridor to a room marked 'Staff only' and gave her a quick look inside. A couple of people were sitting in there, and she recognised one of them as the young woman doctor she had seen a few days ago, talking to the receptionist.

'Dr Imogen Lancaster,' he said, 'and our Registrar, Dr Jason Samuels. This is our new A and E doctor, Saskia Reynolds.' They acknowledged one another with murmured comments and smiles, and then she headed back with Tyler to the main body of the emergency unit.

'Officially, I'm on call this week,' Tyler murmured, 'so it could be a baptism of fire for you. We'll only go out to those cases that the paramedics can't handle, but you'll need to be prepared for that. In the meantime, we'll work through the list of people who've turned up in A and E.' He glanced at the white board that showed the status of patients being seen that morning. 'It looks as though we have someone here who might fit in with your paediatric specialty,' he remarked. 'Tom Carter, in treatment room two, eleven years old. Abdominal pain. Do you want to go and see him while I take a look at the man in the next bay?'

'Okay.' She left Tyler and headed towards the room he had pointed out.

A young boy was lying on the treatment couch, looking feverish and ill, while his mother sat in a chair beside his bed. She was extremely anxious, clasping her hands tightly in her lap, the strain showing in her creased brow and the taut line of her mouth.

A nurse was with them, noting down temperature and blood-pressure measurements on the boy's chart.

Saskia greeted them with a smile and then glanced through the chart the nurse handed to her.

'I hear you're not feeling too good, Tom?' she said, going over to the couch. 'Can you tell me what the matter is?'

'My tummy hurts—and my back—and I

keep feeling sick,' he told her. His eyes were puffy, she noticed, and there was some other facial swelling. From the readings the nurse was taking, she saw that his blood pressure was abnormally high.

'I'll just do a quick examination of your tummy,' she said, 'if that's all right?'

He nodded, and she proceeded to carefully check him over, asking his mother various questions as she did so to try to find out what might be causing his symptoms.

'He's not eating properly,' his mother said, 'and he told me his urine's a dark colour. Do you think there's something wrong with his waterworks?'

'Possibly,' Saskia murmured. 'I'm seeing quite a bit of swelling, which is due to salt and water retention, and that means his kidneys aren't working as well as they should. There could be some inflammation there.' The nurse had done a urine test that showed there was blood in the boy's urine and leakage of protein. They were not good signs.

She listened to the boy's chest and then examined the glands in his neck and asked him to open his mouth so that she could look at his throat. 'We need to do some tests to find out what's causing the problem,' she said, looking over at his mother. 'Some simple blood tests and another urine test. Has he been poorly in the weeks leading up to this?'

'He had a sore throat,' the woman answered. 'We thought it was just a cold and that it would clear up on its own but it seemed to hang on for quite a while.'

'It hurt me to swallow,' Tom put in.

'Yes, your glands are still a bit swollen,' Saskia said. 'I think I'll take a throat swab to see whether you have an infection there that we need to treat.' Tom looked anxious at that and she said hurriedly, 'It's nothing to worry about—I'll use a small cotton wool swab and just gently stroke inside your throat. It won't hurt.'

He relaxed, and she excused herself while she went to find the testing kit. Tyler was standing outside the nearby treatment room, talking to a nurse about his patient, but he broke off when he saw Saskia. 'How's it going? Is everything okay?'

Saskia nodded. 'It's looking as though the boy has a problem with his kidneys and I'm a bit worried about him. There's some swelling to his face and abdomen and he's quite poorly. I'm just going to do a throat swab to see if it's the result of a streptococcal infection.'

He winced. 'That sounds nasty. Okay. Let me know how you go on.'

'I will.'

She went back to her young patient a few minutes later and took a swab from his throat.

'When will we know the results?' his mother asked.

'In a few minutes,' Saskia answered. 'I'll check the swab here and now, but in the meantime I'll organise some medication to help bring down the swelling and get his blood pressure back down to a reasonable level. I think we're going to have to admit him to hospital for a few days so that we can limit his fluids and put him on a special diet to reduce his protein and salt intake.' She wrote out a prescription for the nurse and then went to set up the testing kit to determine the results of the swab.

A short time later she went back to the bedside. 'The swab was positive for a streptococcal infection,' she told the boy's mother, 'so we need to treat that with antibiotics. Does Tom have any problems with taking penicillin? Any allergies at all?'

His mother gave it some thought and then shook her head. 'No, I don't think so.'

'Okay, then. We'll start him on the tablets right away.' She smiled reassuringly at the boy and his mother. 'I know this might be very confusing for you, but if you have any questions at all, we're here to help.'

'Thank you.' The woman clasped Tom's hand in a comforting gesture. 'I'll stay with you, sweetie,' she told him. 'You're going to be all right.'

Saskia left them a few minutes later and

went to the nurses' station to make arrangements to admit Tom to one of the wards. Passing by one of the treatment rooms, she saw Tyler deep in conversation with Dr Lancaster. The woman was smiling up at him, her long, chestnut-coloured hair falling in a silky swathe about her shoulders and swishing gently as she moved her arms to illustrate a point. Tyler grinned at something she said, and a moment or two later he lightly touched her shoulder in a farewell gesture as he made to leave the room.

Saskia hurriedly dragged her gaze away from them, not wanting to be caught staring. All the same, she frowned. Was there something going on between the two of them? Imogen seemed completely at ease with Tyler and he was relaxed and animated in her company.

But why wouldn't he be? she admonished herself a moment later. They must have worked together for some time, and they were obviously friendly with one another. Wasn't that how things should be?

She went to see her next patient, a toddler who was suffering from a respiratory infection, and when she was satisfied that he was comfortable and responding to oxygen treatment and nebulised salbutamol, she headed over to the computer area to type up her notes.

'Hi, there.' Tyler came to stand beside the desk, watching as she entered the details of the medication into the file on screen. 'I hear you've decided to admit the boy with the kidney problem. Is there no way he can be treated at home?'

She shook her head. 'No, or I wouldn't have taken that decision. Why, is there a problem?'

'Not at all. It's just that we only have a few inpatient beds here, so we have to be careful about admissions.'

'I understand that, but I think this child is suffering from acute glomerulonephritis and I don't want to take any risks. He follows all the criteria for admission.'

Perhaps her words came out with more of a sharp edge than she intended, because he said calmly, 'That's okay. You don't need to defend yourself. I was only—'

He broke off as the nurse who had been assisting Saskia earlier hurried towards them. She seemed worried and her tone was urgent. 'I need you to come and take a look at Tom Carter,' she said, looking at Saskia.

'What's wrong, Katie? What's happened?' Tyler was immediately on the alert, already starting towards the treatment room.

'I don't know. He suddenly collapsed. He started to complain of dizziness and feeling faint and his blood pressure has dropped far too quickly. Now he can't get his breath and he's losing consciousness. We're giving him oxygen.'

'All right. That was good thinking.'

Saskia hurried alongside him. What could have gone wrong? She'd made all the necessary checks and was confident in her diagnosis, but there had been nothing in the child's condition that might have led them to expect this sudden deterioration.

Once in the treatment room, though, she could see straight away that Tom was in trouble. White faced, she checked him over, noting that his pulse was weak and his skin was turning a bluish colour. Understandably, his mother was frantic with worry. 'What's wrong with him?' she asked. 'Why is this happening?'

Tyler shot a glance at Saskia and she said huskily, 'He must be reacting to the medication—to the penicillin.'

Tyler nodded agreement. 'He's gone into anaphylactic shock. We need to give him an adrenaline shot, fast.'

Saskia was already preparing the injection, while Tyler pulled up the boy's trouser leg to expose his thigh in readiness.

They waited anxiously for the injection to take effect, and as time went on, Saskia realised that she was holding her breath. This had to work. This had to bring him round.

After what seemed like an age Tom gasped and began to breathe erratically, sucking air wheezily into his lungs.

'He's coming out of it,' Tyler said, beginning to relax a little, 'but I think we should give him a dose of antihistamine and corticosteroids.'

Saskia nodded agreement. She couldn't speak just then. She wanted to, but the words just wouldn't come out. This was her first patient on the first day of her new job and he'd collapsed from something she'd prescribed for him. It was awful to see the boy in this state, and even worse to know that she had unwittingly been the cause of his troubles.

She set up an intravenous line so that Tom could be given the medication he needed. She stayed with him as the drugs began to take effect, and all the time she could hear Tyler talking to the mother, asking about the boy's previous medical history and experience with penicillin.

'Well, he had a chest infection about a year ago,' the woman told him. 'The doctor prescribed penicillin for it. He took the tablets, as he was supposed to, but afterwards he was wheezing more than ever and he said he didn't feel right. We didn't think the antibiotics were working, so we took him back to the GP and he gave him something else to take.'

Tyler nodded, and carefully explained that Tom should never be given penicillin after this reaction. 'He'll need to wear a medic-alert bracelet,' he said, 'and we need to make sure everyone who treats him in the future knows about his sensitivity to the drug. In the meantime, we'll treat him with a different antibiotic.'

By now, Tom was breathing more easily, but was still feeling too unwell to say very much, and when the orderlies came to take him along to his new ward Saskia could do nothing but watch, heart in mouth, as they wheeled him away.

It was a dreadful start to her first day in her new job.

'Shall we go to my office?'

She realised with a jolt that Tyler was waiting for her to go with him. 'Yes, of course.' Things looked bad. The nurse, Katie, was frowning, concerned for the boy, obviously, but could it be that she was wondering if Saskia knew what she was doing?

Saskia followed Tyler to his office. Perhaps she should be grateful that he was considerate enough to talk to her in private about what happened.

'So, tell me about it,' he said, coming straight to the point as they stood and faced each other across the room. He had his back to the window, making a tall, dark silhouette that was framed against the grey, rain-soaked backcloth of the sky. For Saskia, it felt as though the weather was accurately following the course of her mood. 'How did you come to prescribe penicillin if the boy had already had one bad reaction to it?'

'I didn't know about it. His mother didn't mention what happened before.'

'She talked about it just now.'

'Yes, but she must have thought it was his illness that caused him to wheeze and feel unwell, not the tablets, and perhaps the GP didn't pick up on it. I asked her if he was allergic to anything and she said she didn't think so.'

'Okay. Make sure it's written up in his notes, and send a letter to his GP.' He paused briefly. 'Perhaps you'd better let me see your prescription charts for the time being.'

She stiffened. 'You don't trust me to do my job properly?'

He shook his head. 'It's not that. It's just a precaution. I need to have your back—you're new here and people will be looking at everything you do. This is a relatively small community. It's for your own protection.'

'Why would you think I need protecting?' She stared at him fixedly for a moment or two, and saw the darkness come into his eyes. He wasn't doing this because of a one-off adverse reaction, was he? There was more to it than that. He'd had misgivings about her all along, and this was just one more black mark to substantiate his fears. Why was he so cautious about letting her do her job?

'This is Michael's doing, isn't it? That's why

you don't trust me.' She saw the faint widening of his eyes and knew she'd hit the mark. 'What has he said about me now...that I might make mistakes?' She pressed her lips together in a flat line. 'I'm surprised you even let me set foot in this hospital.'

'This latest information came to me after we'd given you the job,' he admitted. 'I spoke to Michael Drew this morning about a patient I transferred over there—a woman who had a bleeding ulcer. It prompted him to mention that you prescribed anti-inflammatories for a patient who subsequently was ill through taking too high a dosage.'

'And I suppose you took that to mean that I'd inadvertently prescribed the wrong dose?' She gritted her teeth. 'It isn't true. I don't suppose he told you that the patient had been buying over-the-counter anti-inflammatories and continued to take them alongside the prescription drug—even though I'd warned him against doing that?'

He shook his head. 'No, he didn't mention that.'

'I'm sure he didn't. Michael's working to his own agenda. The patient thought he was doing himself some good by doubling up on the tablets—that it didn't matter because they were different sorts of anti-inflammatories. He very nearly ended up with a gastric ulcer.'

Tyler went to sit on the edge of the desk. 'So what agenda is your ex-boss following? Why would he want to put obstacles in the way of you keeping this job?'

She gripped the back of a chair, pressing her fingers into the soft leather until her knuckles whitened. 'Who knows what goes on in his mind? Perhaps he's hoping I'll go back to Cornwall and beg for my job back. He didn't want me to leave.'

'That's a very peculiar way for him to behave.' He gave her an assessing look. 'Did you two have some kind of relationship going on?'

'We did…for a while. But it ended when I found out what he was really like. I knew things wouldn't work out for us...but I think I'm only just beginning to see the true extent of his capabilities.'

He sucked in a deep breath. 'I'm sorry this has been going on and that it's causing problems for you. I can see why you might feel the need to be on the defensive...but that's probably all the more reason for me to double-check everything for the time being. It's for your own safety.'

'I don't need protecting,' she said, her green eyes flinty. 'I'm not a junior doctor.'

'All the same, I have overall responsibility for the patients as well as the people on my team, and I think it's important to put controls in place.'

'Then there's nothing more to be said, is there?' She lifted her chin. 'Is that all? Are we done here?'

'Yes, we're done.'

She left his office, angry and upset at the way things had turned out. It didn't matter that he wasn't blaming her...he was acknowledging that other people might. As for Michael, she would have to give him a call and ask him why he was doing this.

'Are you okay?' Katie gave her a concerned look as Saskia went to look in on her next patient. 'You've had a bit of a rough morning, but it could have happened to anyone, you know.'

'I'm fine, thanks, Katie. Or, at least, I will be. Do you know if young Tom is all right?'

Katie nodded. 'I rang the ward to see how he's settling in. I thought you'd want to know. He's responding to treatment—his blood pressure's gone back up towards a more normal level, and he's breathing more easily now.'

'That's good to hear. Thanks for checking up.'

Saskia made a conscious effort to calm down and concentrate on the problems of her next patient, a child who had taken a nasty tumble in the school playground. 'I'm going to have to put a few stitches in this cut,' she told the nurse. 'Would you prepare the suture kit for me?'

'Of course.'

Noah caught up with Saskia around lunchtime as she was leaving one of the treatment rooms.

'Hi, there,' he said with a smile. 'I was hoping you might be about ready for some lunch. Would you let me take you to our restaurant and treat you to something tempting and nutritious? From what I've heard, you might need a bit of pampering.'

'Oh, dear.' Her stomach gave a peculiar lurch. 'Does everyone around here know what's been going on?'

He nodded. 'I'm afraid news travels fast, especially in this place. That's why I bought you these.' With a flourish he produced a posy of flowers from behind his back. 'I thought you might need cheering up.'

Tears stung her eyes. 'That's so thoughtful of you, Noah. Thank you.' She held the beautifully wrapped freesias and breathed in the delicate scent. 'They're lovely—my favourites.'

'Really? I didn't know that. I'm glad you like them.' He crooked his arm and held it out to her. 'Shall we go? They're doing casseroled beef and vegetables as the special today. You're not vegetarian, are you?'

She shook her head. 'No. Just let me put these in water, and I'll be with you.'

'Okay.'

She went to find a vase from near the nurses' station and set the flowers down on the desk where they could be enjoyed by everyone who passed by. Tyler was there, slotting a file in a drawer, and he turned to cast a thoughtful glance in Saskia's direction.

'I wouldn't like you to misconstrue what I'm saying,' he murmured, 'but I think you need to tread carefully. Noah's a good man and a great doctor, but he does have something of a reputation when it comes to women. I'd hate you to jump from the frying pan into the fire.'

'I'll bear it in mind,' she said. Then she walked away from the desk to where Noah was waiting patiently for her, and all the time she was conscious of Tyler's smoke-dark gaze boring into her back.

CHAPTER FIVE

'HOW DID YOUR lunch with Noah go yesterday? Did he manage to make you feel better?' Tyler flicked a sideways glance at Saskia as they drove along the main road towards the coastal town. There was a small frown around his eyes, though whether that was from him needing to concentrate on the road or something to do with her and Noah she couldn't guess. 'I meant to ask you in the afternoon,' he said, 'but things were a bit hectic in the department and on the way home we were too busy discussing other things—it being your first day.'

'And an eventful one at that,' she acknowledged soberly. 'But, yes, it was thoughtful of Noah to try to cheer me up.' She smiled, remembering how Noah had persuaded her to taste a luscious fruit tart and whipped cream and teased her out of her melancholy with tales of his exploits as a junior doctor. 'He can be very entertaining. He made me see that these things happen, things go wrong and I shouldn't take it all personally. I think maybe I've tended to be a bit uptight lately with everything that's happened.'

'That's hardly surprising in the circumstances. You've had to come to grips with an awful lot just lately.'

'Yes.' She looked out of the window, watching the scenery pass by. It was a murky, cold day, with a brisk wind blowing, but nothing could detract from the beauty of the bay with its clear, emerald waters and long stretch of white sand. 'Perhaps I should take more time to appreciate this lovely island.'

'You should. That's a good idea.' Tyler turned the car off the main road and negotiated a maze of streets. 'I often go for a walk by the harbour when I want to clear my head.'

She couldn't imagine him needing to do that.

He always seemed so very much in control of everything. 'I'll try to find time to do that,' she said. They were nearing their destination and that prompted her to ask, 'Who is it that we're going to see today? You mentioned the paramedics were having some difficulty treating a patient.'

'That's right. They were called out to a man who has a heart problem, but he didn't respond to the medication they gave him. We're quite close by so I said I'd come out to look at him.'

He drove along a wide avenue and drew the car to a halt behind an ambulance that was parked by the roadside. Quickly, they gathered up their medical kit and hurried into a small semi-detached house.

'Okay, can you fill me in on what's happening here?' Tyler asked as they approached a paramedic who was frowning at the readout on the defibrillator. Another medic was giving their patient oxygen through a mask.

'This is Simon Jenkins,' the paramedic told

him. 'He was complaining of chest pain, headache and dizziness, as well as feeling sick.'

'Has he actually been sick?'

The paramedic nodded. He frowned, pressing a hand to his temple as though to relieve a throbbing pain. It seemed he, too, wasn't feeling too good. 'He's also short of breath and complaining of difficulty breathing. We've checked out his heart rhythm and it's showing atrial fibrillation, but he's not responding to calcium channel blockers.'

'Okay, thanks.' Tyler knelt down and spoke quietly to Simon, who was fading in and out of consciousness. 'How are you doing, Simon? Can you hear me?' Worryingly, there was only a mumbled response and Tyler began to swiftly check him over.

Saskia went down on her knees beside the man, hastily setting up an intravenous line. Atrial fibrillation meant that the electrical impulses from the heart were disorganised, causing the muscles in the heart to quiver. In turn, this meant the circulation of blood around the body became inadequate, and if this went on for too long there was a strong possibility he could suffer a stroke.

Out of the blue, Simon's limbs started to twitch and Tyler said urgently, 'We need to give him diazepam. He's having a seizure.'

Saskia nodded, but even as she prepared the injection she was thinking about why the drugs he had already been given had not done their job. Something was wrong somewhere. She frowned. Even the paramedics seemed to be out of kilter, as though they were both feeling under the weather. Perhaps it was the heat in the room that was causing the trouble.

She looked around. They were in the living room and because of the chilly morning Simon had lit the wood-burning stove. It burned softly, filling the room with suffocating warmth so that she, too, was beginning to feel lethargic. The room was neat, clean, but near the stove the wall was grubby, with dark, sooty marks spoiling the paintwork. Seeing this, all the connections suddenly came together in her brain.

'Someone needs to switch off the fire,' she said in a brisk, insistent tone. 'I think it could be unsafe, giving off carbon monoxide, and that might be why he didn't respond to the drug he was given earlier.' It was a worrying situation. Once convulsions had started, the man's chances of recovery were dire unless they could counteract the poison—they had to get him out of there, fast.

Tyler was administering the diazepam, but he looked around, suddenly on the alert, and said, 'You're probably right. Let's get him outside into the fresh air—and we need to open the windows in here.'

The paramedics wheeled the man outside, where they went on giving him lifesaving treatment, but after a while Tyler shook his head and said, 'I'm going to call for the air ambulance. At least the seizure's stopped, but his blood pressure's still way too low and his circulation's totally inadequate. The carbon monoxide could have exacerbated the atrial fibrillation, but going on his medical history he's going to need catheter ablation to deal with this heart problem once and for all.' He frowned. 'We'll go with him in the helicopter to try to stabilise him on the journey.'

Saskia nodded, but at the same time her heart gave a small jump. They would be taking Simon to the hospital where her brother and his wife were patients. Might there be a chance she could look in on them while she was over there?

She tried to put those thoughts from her mind while she concentrated on setting up a fluid line to help improve Simon's blood pressure. Tyler was right. None of the measures they were taking would deal with the basic condition that was causing his heart rhythm to go awry. That would only be successfully managed by eliminating the abnormal tissues within his heart, a procedure that had to be done in the electrophysiology suite at the main hospital in Cornwall.

To her relief, the air ambulance touched down close by a few minutes later and they were able to transfer their patient to the well-equipped aircraft.

'You did well back there, picking up on the carbon monoxide,' Tyler said quietly once they were airborne. He checked Simon's vital signs. 'His colour seems to be improving a bit now with the oxygen, but if he'd stayed in that room for just a little longer I think it would have been the end for him. In fact, we might all have been in trouble if you hadn't pointed it out.'

She nodded cautiously, a small shudder going through her at the thought of what might have happened. 'I think it was the heat from the fire that alerted me. I was beginning to feel drowsy, and I couldn't work out why that was happening. Perhaps, being a woman, I'm more susceptible than you and the paramedics.'

'It's possible, though you were closer to the stove than any of us.' He pulled his mobile phone from his pocket. 'I'd better give the police a ring and ask them to sort out some action to make the fire safe or at least stop anyone from using it.'

'Yes, I was thinking of doing that myself—though until today I hadn't realised you could get carbon monoxide poisoning from those kinds of stoves.'

'It can happen if the stove's badly fitted. The gas is formed when wood or any other kind of fossil fuel burns without a good supply of air.'

'I'll bear that in mind if I ever get around to buying one. They're really popular these days.' She looked at Simon and checked the monitor. 'His blood pressure's improving. Hopefully, by the time we get him to the hospital he'll be stable enough to cope with the preparations for the ablation. I expect he'll need to be on blood thinners for a few days before they can do it.'

Tyler nodded. 'You know, since we're going to be at the hospital, you might want to take the opportunity to pay a visit to your brother and his wife.'

Relieved, she smiled at him. 'Thanks for suggesting that. I was wondering if it would be possible for me to go and see them.' It had been thoughtful of him to make the offer. 'I've been feeling quite anxious over the last couple of days,' she admitted. 'Apparently my brother has some kind of infection that's pulling him down, and when I rang yesterday the doctors were quite worried about Megan as well. She's developed some unexpected bruising and swelling to her abdomen. I'd really like to find out what's happening.' She shook her head, as though that would help to rid her of these anxieties. 'I just don't know how I would tell the children if anything were to happen...'

He reached out to her and gently squeezed her hand. The simple gesture melted her heart and made her feel incredibly sorry for herself. Sometimes, over these last few weeks, she'd felt intensely alone, as though her life was one long runaway roller-coaster ride and she was powerless to stop its relentless course. If only she had someone to lean on, someone who might take away some of the burden... It was a foolish, impossible dream, and she was ashamed of herself for succumbing to that moment of weakness.

'It's amazing you've been able to concentrate on anything at all lately,' he said. 'If you need anything at any time, Saskia, or if you just want to talk, I want you to know that I'm here for you. Don't suffer in silence.'

'Thank you.' She was grateful for his consideration, and the warmth and compassion in his touch and in his voice helped to lift her spirits a little. Tyler might not actually be able to do anything to help but she did appreciate his offer.

She stared out of the window and tried to divert her thoughts by gazing down at the craggy Cornish coastline. Soon they were flying over green fields, broken up by wooded valleys, isolated hamlets and the occasional white-painted farmstead. Gradually, as they moved inland, the nature of the landscape changed, with the hamlets giving way to towns, until at last she saw ahead of her the sprawling city of Truro. Any time now they would set down at the hospital where they would offload their passenger.

'Are we all set?' Tyler asked.

'Yes.'

The helicopter landed and they quickly climbed down onto firm ground, handing over their patient to the waiting medical team.

Tyler walked with them to the emergency unit, telling the doctor in charge everything he needed to know about Simon's condition. Saskia followed in his wake. Then they stood back and watched as their patient was wheeled away to the resuscitation room.

'Shall we go and get coffee?' Tyler asked after a while. 'You might want to give yourself a few minutes to compose yourself before you go and see your brother and Megan.'

'That sounds like a good idea.' She looked around the emergency room, a little anxious now that they were in Michael's territory. She certainly didn't want to hang around here any longer than necessary, because every minute meant there was more danger of running into him. Her head felt muzzy and she wasn't in a fit state to deal with him right now.

She'd spoken to him on the phone, wanting to know why he was trying to jeopardise her career, but the answer had been simple. 'I want you back here,' he'd said.

That was never going to happen. It had been bad enough after the accident when Sam and Megan had been brought here. She'd had to liaise with Michael, and that had brought all kinds of tensions to the fore. He hadn't been responsible for saving their lives, but he had been the man in charge and she'd not been able to avoid him initially. She was beginning to bitterly regret ever getting involved with him.

'Are you okay?'

Startled out of her reverie, she looked at Tyler. 'Yes, I'm fine. Coffee would be great. It might help to clear my head—perhaps I'm still suffering some of the effects of the carbon monoxide.'

'Fresh air will help. We'll find a table by an open window.'

They went to the restaurant and Tyler picked out sticky buns to go along with their coffee. 'That should give you a bit of a boost,' he said, smiling as he slid a plate towards her. He stirred brown sugar crystals into his coffee and said cautiously, 'You seemed distracted back in A and E. Were you worried you might come across Michael Drew?'

'Yes, I suppose I was.' She was surprised by his perception. 'Not worried, exactly, but I really don't want to have to deal with him just now.'

He gave her a thoughtful look. 'Had you been dating for some time?'

'About a year. He seemed like a good man, caring and attentive, and at one time I thought we had a good chance of being happy together.' She frowned. 'But he started to become possessive, wanting to know who I was with and where I was going. That was just the beginning of it. Later he tried to tell me what kind of clothes I should wear and how much make-up I should use. He said we needed to spend more time together and tried to stop me from seeing my friends.'

Tyler pulled a face. 'That sounds pretty awful. I'm not surprised you wanted to break free.' He tested his coffee for heat and then took a careful swallow. 'Have you dated anyone since?'

'No. He was the last. After the way things were, I'm not sure I want to get heavily involved with anyone again. It seems to me that relationships are fraught with problems and none of them turn out really well.' She grimaced. 'I should have learned a lesson from my parents' example. Somehow they managed to make a complete mess of things.'

'Oh?' His expression was quizzical. 'What went wrong with them?'

She wriggled her shoulders, as though that would rid her of the disturbing memories. 'I suppose, basically, it was that my father couldn't settle for one woman. His head was easily turned.' Her lips flattened. 'He always made promises, said he was going to change, but he never did, and in the end my mother decided enough was enough.'

'I'm sorry.' His blue gaze was sympathetic.

'That must have been difficult for all of you, not just for your mother.'

'Yes, it was. Sam and I were still young, and we saw my father fairly often at first after he left. But that changed. He couldn't stick to arrangements that had been made. Instead, he'd come up with all sorts of reasons why he hadn't been able to come to a birthday celebration or why at the last minute he couldn't come with us on a trip to the zoo, or whatever.'

'There were a lot of disappointments, then?'

'Yeah.' She took a sip of her coffee. 'Don't get me wrong, I love my father—I just don't have any respect for him. And I think it's taught me to be cautious around men. The experience with Michael just intensified that feeling. I can't say that I hold out any hope for a relationship with long-term stability.'

He frowned. 'But your mother married again, you said. Doesn't that do anything to make you feel better about things?'

She made a wry smile. 'A bit, I suppose, but I can't help seeing her weaknesses—the way

she let my father ride roughshod all over her—
and I don't want to go down that same route.
She's not good at sorting her life out. She used
to look on me as a kind of agony aunt, someone who could help her to work through her
problems. I did what I could, but for myself I
couldn't bear to be tossed this way and that on
a wave of emotional upheaval every time my
love life went wrong. My mother went to pieces
when my father strayed, and I'm not going to
let that happen to me. I know the pain she went
through.'

She bit into the glazed bun, relishing the
sweet, sugar rush of energy that it promised.
She hadn't realised how much she'd needed to
get that outburst off her chest, and now, sur-
prisingly, she felt much better.

She looked up, suddenly very conscious of
Tyler watching her, his gaze lingering on the
moist curve of her lip, and for a moment or two
she floundered uncertainly, licking away any
stray sugar crystals with the tip of her tongue.

He seemed to give himself a mental shake.

'So you have everything under control now, do you? You more or less know where you go from here, how you're going to deal with situations?'

She gave a short laugh. 'Heavens, no. I wish I did. I just get on and deal with stuff and hope I'm doing the right thing. I found out a long time ago that there's no point in making plans if they're going to be constantly overturned.' She put down the bun and licked the stickiness from her fingers. 'All I've ever wanted, really, is to make sure that my brother is okay. We're quite close in age and we turned to one another when we were small and our mother was too busy with her own problems to notice when we needed comforting or cosseting. So we're very close. I need to know that he's going to be all right.'

Tyler studied her briefly. 'It seems to me he's lucky to have a sister like you.'

'Yeah?' She smiled. 'Maybe.' She picked up her bun once more. 'It'll be good to see him today, anyway. I'll try not to keep you waiting for too long.'

'That's okay. I want to check up on Simon and one or two other patients I've transferred recently, just to see how they're doing. And then I'll have to organise the transport back home.'

'Oh…yes, of course. I hadn't thought about that.' She stared at him, a horrible thought creeping into her mind. They wouldn't be flying back, would they? And that left just one way of crossing from the mainland to the island— a way that didn't bode well for her, because her travel sickness pills were in the medicine cupboard back home. It hadn't occurred to her that she might need them at some point today. 'Um…how will we be getting back?'

'I'll book us a couple of seats on a motor launch. They run fairly frequently from the mainland to the islands.'

She was quiet for a while, absorbing that. How on earth was she going to cope with the journey by sea? Car travel she could manage to a point, and the helicopter ride hadn't been too bad, but a sea crossing...no way. She'd always had trouble with boats of any kind.

'Something's on your mind.' Tyler was watching her and his blue gaze missed nothing. 'Out with it. What is it that's bothering you?'

'Um...I get...uh...I have...' She sighed and decided to come right out with it. 'I have a bit of a problem with seasickness. Usually, it wouldn't matter, but unfortunately I...uh... didn't bring my tablets with me today. I wasn't expecting that we'd be going anywhere but locally.'

His eyes narrowed on her thoughtfully. 'I knew there was something you were keeping back at the interview when James mentioned travelling to the off islands. You suddenly went very quiet.'

'I'm sorry.' She sought for a way around the situation. 'It's not usually a problem—I mean, the tablets work well for me...as long as I take them in good time...if I have some warning that I'll be needing to travel, that is. It doesn't mean I can't cope with sea trips.' She frowned. 'Except…maybe today.' She didn't relish the idea of spending two hours or so leaning over the side of the boat with her stomach heaving. It would be unpleasant at best and undignified to say the least. 'I…uh…perhaps I'll be able to sort something out with the pharmacy here.'

'A bit of a problem, you said. How badly do you suffer from it?'

She winced. 'It's pretty bad.'

'Hmm.' He was quiet for a moment or two, thinking things through. 'As you know, most of the travel sickness medications take a while to work, but I could give you an injection. It just means you'll be quite drowsy for a while, and you might even want to sleep, but we can cope with that, I expect.'

The idea of falling asleep while she was with Tyler and supposedly at work didn't appeal at all. She said carefully, 'I think I'd prefer to stick with my usual prescription if you don't mind. Maybe I could take the tablets before I go to see Sam and Megan, and then by the time we go on board the launch I'll be better able to cope.'

'Okay.' He nodded. 'I'll sort it out for you— if I go and get the tablets for you now, you can take them with your coffee.'

'Thanks.' Troubled, she glanced at him. 'Will this make a difference to my keeping this job?'

He made a face. 'It all depends whether we can work out some way of managing the unexpected. Perhaps you could take the tablets as a matter of course when you know we're going to be on call? That way you'll be covered, even if we don't need to use the medical launch.'

'Yes, I could do that.'

'Or you could use a hyoscine skin patch, which will last for up to seventy-two hours. Either way, we'll have to see how the medication affects you. If it makes you too drowsy and unable to think clearly, we might have a problem. We'll just have to wait and see how things work out.'

It wasn't the most encouraging answer but at least he was being honest with her and it was all out in the open at last. She had no idea how things would turn out, but given the start she'd had in this job it was beginning to look as though it would take a miracle for her to keep it.

Tyler left her in order to go over to the pharmacy, but he was back shortly with the tablets and she swallowed them gratefully. 'Thanks,' she said. 'I'm sure I'll be fine now for the journey back.'

He nodded and glanced at his watch. 'You'd better go and see your brother and his wife. I hope things are going better for them by now.'

'So do I.' She hurried away, anxious to know what was happening.

The breath caught in Saskia's throat at the sight of her brother. He was propped up in bed when she went into the intensive care unit, his dark hair spiky against the white pillow. He looked gaunt and his skin was pallid. His eyes were closed and there were rasping sounds coming from his chest.

'He's very breathless,' the nurse told her. 'There's a lot of fluid on his lungs and the doctor's had to put in another chest tube to drain the infection. He's on very strong antibiotics and we're all hoping they'll do the trick, but I'm afraid the doctor is very concerned about him.'

'Thank you for being honest with me. I know you're looking after him really well.'

She went over to her brother and gently squeezed his hand. 'I need you to get better, Sam,' she whispered. 'We're all counting on you to fight this.' He didn't answer, and she guessed he was too exhausted to acknowledge her. He'd been through such a lot of late—a terrible chest injury that had left him fighting for his life, with only the skill of a watchful surgeon to keep him from slipping away. And now this.

She stayed with him for a while, distressed by the sight of all the tubes and wires that were attached to him. As a doctor, she knew why they were there, what they were for, but it was heartbreaking to see someone she loved in such a vulnerable state.

'The children are always asking about you and they send you their love,' she told him. 'They've made some cards and presents to bring with them next time they come here. Please try to get better. We need you.'

After a few minutes, when the doctor came to administer medication via the catheter in Sam's hand, Saskia left his bedside and went to find Megan.

Her sister-in-law was in an equally poor condition and Saskia was more worried than ever when she saw the monitor readings.

'What's caused her to go downhill like this?' she asked the nurse. 'Has she been bleeding internally?' The bruising and swelling both pointed to that as a reason for Megan's problems.

'I'm afraid so,' the nurse answered. 'The tests we took yesterday revealed a leak from one of the pelvic blood vessels. She's had surgery to put it right, but it looks as though there's another problem to worry about—an abscess has formed.'

Saskia grimaced. That was very bad news, coming on top of all her injuries, and the chances of Megan making a good recovery were lessening by the hour. 'But they've put in a drainage tube?'

'Yes.' The nurse nodded. 'And she's receiving antibiotics to try to stop the infection.'

'Okay. That's good… Thank you.'

None of it was good, though, and Saskia left the unit feeling deeply unhappy. Megan was a lovely, sweet-natured young woman, who made everyone around her feel better. To see her suffering like this was soul-destroying.

Her eyes were bright with unshed tears. By now she'd hoped and prayed that both Sam and Megan would be starting to heal and would be showing signs of recovery, but that prospect seemed further away than ever. It was heartbreaking to see them this way.

'You've no colour in your face at all,' Tyler commented when she met up with him by the main entrance to the hospital a few minutes later. He looked concerned as he studied her bleak expression. 'Was it bad—worse than you expected?'

She nodded, unable to find her voice just then.

'Perhaps you should sit down for a while,' he said. 'There's a bench seat over there, where we can be private.' He led her to a quiet, land-scaped corner of the hospital grounds, set back in a green, wooded area to one side of the car park.

She sat down and as he came to sit beside her he searched her face closely once more. 'Are you warm enough? You're looking really peaky.'

Her shoulders lifted almost imperceptibly. She didn't know what she felt just then. She felt numb inside.

'They're both fighting for their lives,' she whispered. Tears began to slowly spill down her cheeks. 'Right now, I don't even know if they're going to make it.'

'I'm sorry,' he said. He put his arms around her and drew her to him, cradling her head against his chest. She felt the warmth of his body seep into her, and the firmness of his embrace was deeply comforting, shoring her up and giving her the strength that she needed to go on.

'I couldn't bear it if anything were to happen to Sam,' she whispered. 'He's everything to me. And Megan—we're like sisters… How would I cope without them?'

'Don't think like that,' he said softly. 'You need to be strong, for yourself and for the children. They mustn't see that you have any doubts. You're all they have.'

'But what if I can't do it?' The anguish showed in her face and he lifted a hand to gently caress her cheek.

'Of course you can do it. I've seen the way you are with those children, and you won't let them down. You'll do whatever's necessary.'

'You seem so certain of that.' Her mouth

trembled and she looked at him through tear-drenched eyes. 'I w-wish I could b-be so sure.'

He moved closer, and it was clear her distress had had a profound effect on him. 'You're not on your own in this,' he said huskily. 'I'm here for you. I promise you, Saskia, I'll help you through it, any way I can.' His gaze lingered on the soft, vulnerable curve of her mouth and slowly, as though he simply couldn't help himself, he bent his head and gently claimed her lips.

The kiss was tender and sweetly seductive, easing her troubled soul like an exquisite soothing balm. He gave a soft, shuddery sigh, as though he'd fought a battle within himself and lost, and now he was like a man drowning in need.

She, too, lost herself in that kiss, in his comforting arms, in the hands that caressed her and invited a response. She was safe here, nothing bad could happen because he was holding her and he would keep the world at bay. It was like an unspoken promise that hung on the air between them.

He stroked her hair, his fingers sliding into the silky curls at the nape of her neck. 'You'll get through this,' he said, his voice threaded with emotion. 'Please, don't cry. You'll be all right.' He held her as though he would take all of her pain away. 'I hate to see you hurting like this...but you will overcome all these hurdles. I know you will—somehow we'll get through it, together.'

He couldn't know that things would turn out all right, could he? But she nodded faintly, accepting his reassurances, wiping the dampness from her cheeks with the tips of her fingers.

He cared about her enough to want to protect her, to help her to feel better, and for a few moments he had succeeded. She had been able to cast it all aside and think of nothing but him.

She carefully eased herself away from him and he watched her slowly straighten up. He moved towards her, edging closer, as though some inner compulsion was urging him to take her in his arms once more, but at the last moment he stopped himself. He seemed wary all at once, guarded, and locked in conflict with himself. She didn't know what to make of him. Was he already regretting his actions?

He hesitated before saying what needed to be said. 'I shouldn't have kissed you,' he said quietly. 'I should have known better, should have had more self-control. I'm your boss, your mentor, so to speak, and I overstepped the mark. I'm sorry, really sorry.'

'It's all right,' she murmured. 'I shouldn't have let my feelings show...we were both caught off guard. I was a bit off balance for a while, but I'm all right now.'

She wasn't all right, of course. Her lips still tingled from his kiss. Those few blissful moments in his arms had been wonderful, and for just a little while he had managed to blot everything from her mind.

But it should never have happened. He was right about that. That kiss had been extra-special, incredibly moving, tender and full of

promise, but it wasn't right for them to have explored their feelings for one another that way.

It would be a mistake to get involved with
anyone from her place of work, and especially
with him, wouldn't it? He'd already said he was
finding it difficult to reconcile his professional
obligations with his feelings towards her.

It wouldn't be fair to either of them to let their
emotions get out of hand, would it?

But wasn't it already too late?

CHAPTER SIX

'IS EVERYTHING ALL right between you and Tyler?' Noah came into the staffroom and saw Saskia standing by the coffee maker.

'Um…' Saskia thought about that for a moment or two. 'Yes, I think so,' she answered cautiously. She frowned. How had Noah managed to pick up on their difficulties? Hadn't she and Tyler been ultra-careful around one another ever since the day he'd kissed her? In fact, Tyler seemed to be going about his work in a perfectly normal fashion—she was the one who was finding things difficult.

'Why?' she asked Noah. 'What makes you think there's a problem?'

He shrugged lightly and helped himself to biscuits from the cookie jar. 'He's been quite tense these last few days, and that isn't like him at all.' He frowned. 'I suppose it could be that his plans for the house aren't going too well.'

'Plans? What plans?'

'Oh, you haven't heard about them? He wants to remodel the interior of his house to make it more light and open, but he isn't too sure yet how to go about it. I think he feels everywhere's too cluttered at the moment.' He smiled. 'It isn't, of course, not by normal people's standards, but Tyler likes everything to be streamlined, very neat and everything in its place. It's a thing with him. He's the same with the garden.'

He propped himself up against the worktop, facing her. 'You must know what he's like by now. Everything has to be faultless...a bowling-green lawn and manicured flower borders. Even the trees and the shrub garden are pruned to conform to his idea of perfect symmetry. And have you seen his small patch of kitchen garden? It looks as though it's been planted out along regimental lines.'

'Oh, dear.' Saskia paused, holding the coffee

jug motionless in mid-air. 'Yes, I'd noticed his beautiful garden. These things are important to him, aren't they?' Absently, she poured coffee into her cup. 'I'm afraid I'm probably to blame if he's not himself of late. I might have upset the apple cart.'

He looked at her askance. 'How? Why? What could you have done? It's certainly not your work—people speak very highly of you.'

'Well, that's a relief.' She pulled a face. 'Although I still think Tyler's waiting for me to trip up somehow. But actually it's nothing to do with work.' She placed the coffee jug back on its stand. 'The thing is, the children and I took Boomer for a walk the other day, and I let him off the lead as we came back towards the house—as I always do. Usually there's not a problem, he'll wait for me by the front door... but not this time. He must have picked up a scent of some sort because he took off at top speed and before I could stop him he'd dashed into Tyler's back garden.'

'That doesn't sound good.'

'No.' Her mouth turned down at the corners. 'There were a couple of loose slats in one of the fence panels—well, to be honest, I think Boomer was responsible for those in the first place. Whenever the postman calls Boomer tries to head butt his way out of the garden and onto the side path.'

She frowned. 'Anyway, he managed to get through the other day. Of course, I went after him—through the gate, not the fence,' she added hastily, and Noah's mouth curved. 'I'd no idea what was going on, or what he was after. But then the children admitted that some-one—probably Charlie, though he wouldn't own up to it—had left the rabbit's cage un-done and Bugsy had escaped about an hour earlier. They'd looked everywhere apparently, but couldn't find him.'

'Uh-oh…this is getting worse by the second.' Noah grinned as he took a cup down from the shelf. 'I suppose the rabbit had managed to find his way into Tyler's garden as well?'

She nodded. 'Oh, yes. By the time I caught

up with him he'd had a whale of a time, eating his way through the carrots and peas, and when Boomer started chasing him the pair of them ran amok in the flower beds. The chrysanthemums and the dahlias were trampled into the ground. I felt awful.'

Noah tried unsuccessfully to suppress a smile. 'Oh, dear. What did Tyler have to say about that? I'd love to have seen the look on his face.'

Saskia's mouth twitched a fraction. 'He didn't say very much at all, to be honest. When Boomer started barking Tyler came out of the house and asked what was going on, but once he'd taken in what was happening I don't think he could trust himself to speak. He grabbed Bugsy and put him back in his cage and then he just glared at the dog. I've a feeling he wanted to grab him by the scruff of the neck and shake him, but he managed to hold back. I'd been trying to catch Boomer all this time, but he thought it was a game and kept running off. Tyler was too quick for him, though. He just grabbed him by his collar and marched him over to me.'

'He must have said *something* to you.' Noah pushed his cup towards her on the worktop and she filled it with hot coffee.

She made a wry smile. 'Yes…well, he did say a few choice words between gritted teeth. The gist of it was along the lines of "How long was this tenancy supposed to last?" and then he muttered something under his breath. I didn't catch it all, but I think the end product might have been "There has to be some way the agreement can be broken."' She rolled her eyes. 'I'm hoping he didn't mean it. I did say that we would go over to his place and try to put the damage right as far as possible, but he looked horrified at the thought. I'm sure he expected us to make matters worse.'

Noah laughed. 'I wouldn't take it to heart. I've never known Tyler to lose his self-control or stay annoyed for too long. This will all blow over soon enough.'

'Hmm, maybe, but I wish there was something I could do to put things right. I'm wondering if I should offer to help him out with his plans for the house. If he's having trouble visualising them, I might be able to come up with a solution.'

'It could be worth a try.' Noah sipped his coffee. 'I know Imogen spends quite a bit of time at his place, but she obviously hasn't been able to come up with anything. She's pretty much like him—she's very organised. I think she suggested taking out some of the furniture and removing a bookshelf here and there, but he didn't seem too keen on that idea.'

Saskia's brow furrowed. Imogen—Dr Lancaster—seemed to be the one person Tyler trusted. He was always pleasant to her and seemed to be in a good mood whenever she was around. But, then, Imogen probably never put a foot wrong. She was always perfectly groomed, her hair was sleek and smooth, and she ran her cardiovascular clinic with flawless efficiency. She was probably Tyler's ideal woman. A wave of depression rolled over her.

'Does that bother you—about Imogen seeing Tyler outside work?' Noah's voice cut into her thoughts and she came back to earth with a bump.

'I…I'm not sure,' she hedged, aware that he was watching her carefully. 'Maybe. A bit.' She didn't want to own up to her true feelings, but Noah seemed to see quite easily through her subterfuge.

'You've fallen for him, haven't you?' His mouth made a rueful shape. 'Perhaps I should have guessed before this.'

'I don't know what I feel,' she murmured. 'I'm not looking to get involved with anyone.'

'No, maybe not.' He gave her a wry smile. 'I had the feeling I wouldn't get anywhere with you…but I'm here for you, you know, any time you need a friend.'

'Thanks, Noah.' She stroked his arm lightly. 'And I do appreciate you listening to me. You've been a great help.' She hesitated. 'I'm sorry if you had any other expectations.'

'Don't worry about it.'

She went to rinse out her cup at the sink. 'I'd better get back to work,' she said. No doubt he would work his charm on some other young woman. It was his nature not to be down-hearted for too long.

And at least he'd given her an idea as to how she could make things up to Tyler. She left him to his coffee and went back to A and E.

'Would you come and take a look at the woman in room four?' Katie asked as soon as she saw Saskia. 'I'm worried about her. She's complaining of nasty chest pain and aching in her jaw, but according to the ECG readout there's no sign of a heart attack. She has a history of high blood pressure and she keeps feeling faint.'

'Okay, I'll come right away.'

Saskia followed Katie into the treatment room and could see at once that the woman was in a great deal of pain, too restless even to sit comfortably on the bed. She was in her late forties, with dark hair that clung damply around her face. Katie was encouraging her to breathe oxygen through a face mask but she put that briefly to one side to answer Saskia's questions.

'Can you tell me what happened?'

'I've been feeling ill for a few days.' She was clearly breathless. 'I thought it might be flu, but then I started to get this pain in my jaw. It's a horrible, throbbing pain. But the pain in my chest is the worst.'

Saskia nodded. 'Can you describe it?'

'It's unbearable. It was like a ripping, tearing sensation, and now…now it's really awful, the worst ever.' She paused to get her breath, and Saskia quickly ran the stethoscope over her chest.

'All right, Mrs Miller—Jenny…' She smiled at her. 'I'll give you something stronger for the pain, and I'm going to arrange for you to have X-rays and a CT scan.' Jenny's blood pressure was dropping, and while that would be a good sign in someone who was usually hypertensive, in this case Saskia felt it was something else entirely.

'It's bad, isn't it?' Jenny slumped against her pillows. Her features were grey and drawn with anxiety and beads of perspiration had broken out on her brow. 'Am I going to die?'

Saskia laid a hand on her shoulder. 'You're very poorly, but nothing bad is going to happen to you while I'm looking after you.' She was almost tempted to cross her fingers behind her back as she said that. If what she suspected was true, this woman was in real, life-threatening danger. Above all, she had to keep her from becoming severely stressed. 'In the meantime, I just want you to rest and not worry about anything.'

Jenny nodded wearily and went back to gulping oxygen through the breathing mask.

As soon as she had arranged for a porter to take Jenny along to Radiology, Saskia went in search of Tyler. Katie was right to be concerned about this patient—something dire was going on here and if her tentative diagnosis was correct they would have to act super-fast. Jenny's life could be at stake.

She found Tyler in one of the other treatment rooms and as she entered he looked up, sending her an oblique glance. 'Is something wrong?' he asked, and she nodded.

'Okay, give me a minute.' He finished checking his patient's reflexes and then asked the nurse to admit the man to the observation ward.

Stepping out of the treatment room, he gave Saskia a narrowed look, and she guessed he thought it unusual that she should come in search of him. So far, whenever possible, she had tried to sort out any problems for herself without involving him. She'd wanted to show him that she didn't need to be constantly monitored, that she was perfectly capable of acting independently.

Now, though, she was afraid this was something she couldn't deal with on her own. Jenny would need expert surgical intervention.

'What's the problem?' he asked. His manner was brisk and professional, and she found herself missing his former friendly approach.

'My patient is very seriously ill, and I don't

believe we can treat her here, in this hospital. I think we need to call out the air ambulance.'

'Uh-huh. Tell me more.'

Quickly, she outlined Mrs Miller's condition. 'She isn't showing the symptoms of a heart attack, but I'm afraid it could be far worse.'

He frowned. 'There are several things it could be—an ulcer, gallstones. They can cause severe pain. We wouldn't need to call out the helicopter for those.'

'But she does have a heart murmur. What if it's a tear in the aorta? That's a possibility, too, isn't it? She described a tearing pain.' The aorta was the heart's major blood vessel and anything going wrong with that could have dreadful consequences.

'Hmm…do you think you might be making too much of this? People's descriptions of pain aren't necessarily accurate. It's all subjective.'

She stood her ground. 'Either way, it will show up on the CAT scan. I think you need to come and look for yourself.'

'You've had the results already?' He started to walk with her to the radiology unit.

'Not yet, but I'm fairly certain they'll show a problem with the artery. If we're lucky it has only just started leaking—that could be why her blood pressure is dropping. If not, she might only have a few hours left.'

He frowned. 'You seem very sure about this.'

'I've seen it before. That's how I've learned to be on the lookout for it.'

They went into the CAT scan booth and after studying the films on the monitors for a few minutes Tyler made a whistling sound through his teeth. 'There's an aneurysm—here, do you see? The artery's blown at a weak spot—probably due to the persistently high blood pressure.'

He moved away from the screens and spoke briskly. 'Okay, let's put in a couple of large-bore IV lines and get her started on beta blockers to reduce the forces on the arterial wall. We'll keep her on morphine for the pain.'

'I'll see to it.'

'Good. I'll alert the hospital in Truro that they need to have a team standing by.'

She nodded and hurried away, immensely relieved that he had listened to her. Her priority now was to prevent the tear in the artery from getting any worse.

By the time Tyler came back to her a few minutes later, she had done everything she could to stabilise their patient. 'Will we be going with her in the helicopter?' she asked, but he shook his head.

'They're sending over one of their cardiac specialists to stay with her on the journey. She'll go for surgery to repair the damage as soon as they arrive back at the hospital.' He studied her with renewed respect. 'That was well spotted. You might just have saved her life.'

'I hope so.'

Tyler spoke to Jenny for a while, reassuring both her and her husband, who had arrived at her bedside in a state of great anxiety. He promised them both that she would be well looked after. He answered all their questions and Saskia could see that they felt comforted by his compassionate, capable bedside manner. Then, when he judged they needed some time to talk things through, he excused himself and left them in the care of the nurse.

He walked with Saskia to the nurses' station. 'How are things with you? Have you heard anything more from the hospital about your brother and his wife?'

'There's been no real change,' she told him. 'The doctors have identified the specific bacterium causing Sam's infection and they're trying him on a different antibiotic. They've put him on diuretics to try to reduce his fluid load, but so far it's still an uphill struggle. It's much the same with Megan, too. The abscess doesn't seem to be responding to treatment, so they're having to try other drugs.'

'I expect it will take some time before you see any real results. At least things are no worse. Perhaps that's something to bear in mind.'

'Yes, I suppose so.'

He gave her a quick, cautious glance. 'If you need any help with getting over there to see them, I could arrange things for you with a friend who has a motor launch. I know how expensive it can be on the ferry. He'll just need to know when exactly you plan to travel.'

'Thanks, I appreciate that.' Grateful, she laid a hand fleetingly on his arm, needing that brief moment of intimacy. He gave her shoulder a light squeeze in return.

'Any time. I'll do whatever I can.'

Despite the tension between them, he was keeping his word about helping her, and she appreciated that. He was a thoughtful, considerate man, and she didn't want to put up barriers between them. Even in the short space of time she'd known him she'd found herself looking for him, at home and at work, wanting to be near him.

She couldn't forget that kiss, the way he'd held her. It had been something special, deliciously tender, and even now she went hot all over at the thought of it.

It wouldn't do, of course. She was tormented by the knowledge that falling for someone like him could only ultimately lead her to pain and heartbreak. If they started a relationship and things went wrong between them she would be the one to pay the price. Her working life would become a nightmare.

If she didn't want to go through the problems she'd had with Michael all over again, she had no choice but to put up a wall of sorts between them.

The air ambulance arrived within a few minutes and she went with Tyler to hand over their patient to the specialist doctor. 'We have a team waiting, ready to operate,' the doctor said. 'We'll keep you informed, but judging by the scans you sent us she'll be in surgery for several hours.'

'Okay, thanks.' Tyler waited near to the helipad, watching as the aircraft took off. 'We should know one way or another by this evening,' he said, giving Saskia a quick, sidelong glance.

'Yes. I hope she makes it.'

Back at home later that day Saskia was on edge, waiting for news. Spotting Tyler out in the garden, doing what he could to tidy up the flowerbeds, she decided to go over to the fence to talk to him. Maybe he'd heard something.

'I haven't, not yet.' He finished staking and tying up the chrysanthemums and then straightened, looking around as he heard laughter and shouts coming from behind her. Becky and Charlie were playing cricket in the garden.

'They seem to be enjoying the fresh air.'

'Yes, I've been trying to encourage them to play outside more.' She'd pushed some cricket stumps into the lawn, hammering them into place, and the children were having great fun taking it in turns with the bat and ball. It only occurred to her now, as she watched them running about, that the once unspoiled grass was becoming worn down by the steady tramp of children's feet. What would Tyler think of that?

Swallowing down on her guilt, she tried to

push those thoughts to the back of her mind and said, 'Actually, they're going off in about half an hour on a camping weekend. Some teachers from the school are taking quite a few of the children to explore the wildlife and natural vegetation of the island. It's part of a school project.'

'Are they looking forward to it?'

'I think so. I'm the one who's not so sure. I'll miss them.'

He smiled. 'Yes, I suppose you were bound to get attached.' His expression sobered as his glance moved over the house and garden and she wondered if he was imagining a different set of people living there...a couple without small children and pets perhaps?

'Do you still regret letting out your property?' she asked. 'I'm sorry about what happened the other day with the fence and the plants—but I suppose if you have tenants there are always going to be problems of some sort.'

'That's probably true,' he acknowledged. 'No, on the whole, I don't have any regrets.'

That was a bit of a relief, at least. 'How did you get into the property business?'

'By accident, I suppose. I inherited my house from my grandparents—my father's parents. I didn't need to live in it to begin with because I was working in another town, so that's when I first thought of renting it out. And then later I bought the property next door when it came on the market.'

She frowned. 'How is it that the house didn't go to your father?'

'He'd already died of a heart attack. So the property went to me and my sister—I offered to buy out Suzie's half and she was happy to go along with that.'

She looked at the mellow stone building with its Georgian-style windows. 'It's a beautiful old house.'

'Yes, it is. It needs work, some modernising, but it's solid, and I'm happy with it.'

She said curiously, 'It must have been difficult for your mother when your father died—

for all of you. I would imagine you were fairly young at the time.'

'It's always upsetting when someone dies.' He pulled in a sharp breath. 'But, to be honest, life was never easy when he was around. He spent his time chasing dreams, starting up one failed business venture after another. For us, it meant that there was never enough money, and we were always moving from one place to another, following his schemes. We were never able to put down roots.'

'I'm sorry.' She was shocked. She'd always imagined that everything in his life had gone smoothly for him. 'I'd no idea. It must have been so hard for you.'

He shrugged. 'It was unsettling more than anything. You never knew what was around the corner, how long you'd be able to stay at the same school, whether you'd have to say goodbye to your friends and try to make new ones. But children do tend to adapt to circumstances fairly easily—I think it was much harder for my mother. She constantly had to start afresh, and after he died she was lost and vulnerable. I felt it was up to me to look after her and Suzie.'

Saskia absorbed all that, studying the varying emotions that crossed his face as he spoke. What part had his troubled childhood played in his continuing search for order in his life? It all seemed to make sense now.

'Saskia—' Caitlin burst in on her train of thought, coming over to where she was standing by the fence. She was rubbing her neck as though it ached, and at the same time she wriggled her shoulders as if that might ease discomfort of some sort.

'Are you all right?' Saskia asked. 'Do you have a neck ache?'

'It's just a muscle pain. I've got a bit of a headache—but I'll be fine. Perhaps I'll take a couple of painkillers…'

'Yes, okay. That sounds like a good idea.'

Caitlin came closer, saying quietly, 'I just thought that if Becky and Charlie are going away this weekend, would it be all right if I go and have a sleepover with a friend from school? You've met her—it's Gemma, the one who lives on a farm.'

Saskia lifted a doubtful brow. 'Are you sure you're up to it if you're not feeling well?'

'I'm fine. I really want to do this.'

Perhaps it would do her good to get away from the house for a while. 'Well, all right, then, if you're sure. Are your friend's parents okay with it?' Caitlin nodded, and Saskia added, 'Make sure you ring me if you change your mind and want to come home again. And you'd better give me Gemma's home phone number just in case.'

Caitlin bridled at that. 'So you don't trust me?'

Saskia put an arm around her, trying to calm her down. She sensed Tyler watching the exchange with interest...why was it she had so much difficulty dealing with Caitlin? She wanted to do the right thing, but somehow she always managed to strike sparks. 'Of course I trust you. It's just a precaution, in case I need to get in touch with them for any reason. I want to know you're safe.'

'Hmmph. Okay, I suppose. I'll go and get ready.' Caitlin turned away and walked quickly back to the house.

'She's not too happy, is she?' Tyler murmured. 'Is this the typical moody teenager syndrome?'

'I'm not sure.' Saskia stared thoughtfully after her. 'She's anxious about her parents, of course, and I think she's missing her friends from back home. She was settled in Cornwall and it's taking her a while to adjust to the move. I suggested they talk to one another via video chat. I'm pleased she's found new friends over here, though. It's a good start.'

'It is.' He studied her briefly. 'If you're going to be on your own this evening, perhaps you'd like to come over to my place for supper? I can't promise anything special—I don't do a lot of cooking—but I was planning on making pizza. It's simple enough that even I can do it. There's no point in both of us cooking, is there?'

Her heart gave a small lurch of anticipation at the prospect of spending time with him, but at the same time she was at war within herself. Should she accept his offer? Oughtn't she to steer clear of invitations like this one? The instinct of self-preservation kicked in and was nudging her, telling her that she should turn him down…but a wilful, tempestuous streak fought back. Did she really want to spend an evening by herself when he was just next door?

'I'd like that,' she said.

'Good.' He smiled. 'Give me half an hour or so to get freshened up?'

'Okay.'

She made sure Becky and Charlie had everything they needed for their weekend away, and then waved them goodbye when their driver came to pick them up. 'Have a good time,' she told them.

Caitlin had packed an overnight bag with hair straighteners, pyjamas and a change of underwear, and as soon as she had set off for the bus stop Saskia went to get changed.

She pulled on blue skinny jeans and a pretty beaded top, and spent a few minutes applying a light touch of make-up. She was looking forward to being with Tyler. In spite of all her misgivings and inner warnings, she wanted to be with him.

'Hi,' she said, when he opened the front door to her a short time later. 'Am I too early?'

'Of course not.' His gaze swept over her, his blue eyes appreciative. 'You look lovely,' he said.

Inside, she fizzed with elation at the compliment. 'Thanks.' He looked pretty good himself, in dark, beautifully cut trousers and a short-sleeved designer top.

He took a step back. 'Come in.' The hallway opened up to a closed-in staircase on one side, and further along the hallway a door led into a large lounge/dining room. 'This is the main room of the house,' he said, 'the one where I spend most of my leisure time—except for the kitchen, of course.'

She looked around. It was a high-ceilinged

room, with tall Georgian windows and a beautiful feature fireplace. 'This is lovely,' she said. 'You've kept all the original features in here.' She daren't even think about what would happen if the children were let loose in this house. And as for Boomer…

'Yes, I wanted to keep the character of the place. It feels a bit oppressive to me, though, and I'd like to do something to modernise it and add some light.'

She nodded. 'Noah told me…he said you weren't sure what to do. I think it's really elegant.' The furniture was simple, minimal, even, but what there was had a classic, timeless feel to it.

He sent her a quick glance. 'You and Noah seem to be getting on pretty well…'

'Yes, he's easy to talk to.'

His mobile phone warbled just then and he said quickly, 'Excuse me. It might be the hospital.' He checked the display. 'Yes, it is.' He connected the call and listened carefully for a minute or two. 'All right, thanks for letting me know.'

'Is it Jenny Miller?' Saskia asked when he'd slipped his phone back into his pocket. 'Did she come through the operation okay?'

'Yes, she did. Obviously, she's still in Intensive Care, and they're concerned about her blood pressure and respiration, but at least she came through the surgery.' He sent her a long, assessing look. 'If it hadn't been for you noticing the signs, it's quite likely she might not even have reached that far.'

She breathed a sigh of relief. 'I'm really glad for her.' A high percentage of people didn't survive when they suffered a tear in the main artery, so the fact that Jenny had been able to undergo surgery was a huge blessing—and a great weight off her mind. 'That's wonderful news.'

'It is.' He reached for her and gave her arms a gentle squeeze. They stood there for a while, not moving, simply basking in the moment, until at last Tyler pulled himself together and said, 'Come on, let me show you the rest of the house. The kitchen's through here. The food should just about be ready.'

Still glowing inside from his thoughtful, tender embrace, she followed him out of the room.

The kitchen was warm, filled with the appetising smell of the pizza that was baking in the classical white-painted Aga. There was a large free-standing island unit in the middle of the room, painted a gentle cream colour, with drawers and cupboards in slatted wood, and around the walls were various bespoke pieces in a pleasing mixture of white and cream. To one side of the room, facing the wide window, there was a deep porcelain sink, and further along, near the glass doors that opened out on to a patio, there was a hand-crafted table and chairs.

'This is perfect,' she said, gazing around in awe. 'Why would you want to change anything in here?'

He looked surprised. 'I don't, particularly. I had this room renovated a couple of years ago, so it's probably the best room in the house. It's the rest I'm concerned about. I don't know how best to make changes without spoiling the original features of the house.'

'Perhaps you don't need to do much.' She helped him to set the table, putting out plates and cutlery, a bowl of salad and bread sticks. There was a warm intimacy to sharing the simple domestic tasks, and more than once she had to pull her attention back to their conversation. 'The curtains in the living room are quite heavy looking,' she murmured. 'You might want to change them for something much lighter in texture and colour, and maybe change the wall colour to something pale with just a hint of warmth.'

He waved her to a chair. 'You think that would make much of a difference?' He sounded doubtful as he drew the pizza from the oven and transferred it to a circular board. Next to that, he set down a plate of hot barbecued chicken wings.

'I do. I think you'll be surprised at the result.

It might also lighten things up if you add two or three cushions—perhaps a pale green and cream silk would look good.'

'I might try that. Like you say, it wouldn't take much, but it could change the whole atmosphere of the room.' He gestured towards the food spread out on the table. 'Help yourself,' he said, coming to sit opposite her, 'but be careful—it's hot.' He started to cut the pizza into triangular wedges, then wiped his hands on a serviette and began to pour wine into two crystal wine glasses.

She watched his deft, supple movements, and then took a quick sip of wine to cover her uncertainty. There was something about his long, lithe body that made her senses quiver in anticipation.

'Thanks,' she murmured. 'It smells delicious. I didn't realise how hungry I was.' She bit into the pizza, savouring the melted cheese and luscious peppers. It was mouth-wateringly good and as she lifted her little finger to wipe a faint line of moisture from her lower lip, she looked up to see that Tyler was watching her with rapt attention.

'Pizza makes a tasty meal,' she said awkwardly, feeling self-conscious, 'but it's not always easy to eat it with any kind of elegance.'

'Oh, I don't know about that,' he murmured. 'It looks pretty good from where I'm sitting.'

Warm colour flowed along her cheekbones. 'Um...about the house,' she said huskily, searching for a way back to safe ground, 'perhaps you could open up the staircase in the hall—take off the wooden boards that have been used to enclose it and expose the spindles. It would give a completely different feel to that part of the house.'

He thought about that. 'You're very good,' he said, giving her a shrewd look. 'How do you know these things?'

She smiled. 'Well, I have to confess my mother has her own interior design business—she's always trying out new ideas, and I think over the years some of her knowledge must have rubbed off on me.'

'Ah…that explains it.' He picked up a chicken wing and bit into it. 'I expect it's in your blood.'

'Maybe.' It was fascinating to watch him eat, to see those strong, capable fingers curled with such finesse around a morsel of food. He licked the sauce from his thumb and forefinger, and then paused to study her thoughtfully once more. 'Are you okay?'

'Uh…yes, I'm fine.' She bent her head to add a helping of salad to her plate.

'I think you said you don't see too much of your parents—have they been to visit your brother and Megan? You haven't mentioned it.'

'Yes, they've been to see them a few times. My mother commutes—she has to leave someone else in charge of the business while she's away, but she always has her laptop with her so that she can keep an eye on things. And my father has flown over from Spain a couple of times.' She wiped her fingers on a serviette and then rested her hand by her wine glass. 'They're very worried.'

'I'm sure they must be.' He laid his hand on

hers and gave her a long, thoughtful look. 'It's hard on all of you, but you seem to be managing to keep it all together. I think you're doing an amazing job with the children. It can't have been easy to take them on.'

'Thanks.' She smiled, comforted by the warm reassurance of his gentle touch. It took away all the loneliness of her situation. 'I've always been involved with them from the day they were born. They're the next best thing to having a family of my own.' She studied him in return. 'What about you? Do you ever think about having a family of your own one day?'

He was silent for a moment, reluctantly releasing her hand and frowning as he turned his attention back to his meal. 'I haven't given it a lot of thought,' he said at last. 'I suppose I'm used to the solitude of this house.' He smiled. 'Or at least I *was*. It's something else to think of a horde of youngsters running around the place. I'm not averse to it, but it would take some getting used to, I think.'

'Perhaps it's different if they're your own.'

'Maybe.'

Deep down she might have been hoping for a different kind of answer, but she really ought to have known better. Tyler was used to perfection in everything. He'd moulded his life to the pattern he wanted, and he wasn't likely to change that any time soon, was he? Why did that bother her so much?

'I think I ought to give Caitlin a call and see if she arrived safely at her friend's house,' she said, anxious to shift the conversation to less controversial ground. 'She should be there by now.'

He nodded. 'I'll get the dessert.'

'Oh, I'm sorry.' She looked at him in dismay. 'I'll phone her later. I didn't realise you'd made a dessert as well.'

'No, no. Go ahead and make the call. It's important.' He gave her a quick smile before going over to the fridge and taking out two glass dishes. 'I must confess the dessert is the simplest I could think of—fruit salad with cream.'

'Mmm…my favourite, next to blackberry and apple crumble.' She smiled as he speared a pineapple chunk with a fork and let it float in the air irresistibly close to her mouth. 'Oh, bliss.' She bit off the sweet fruit and let the juice trickle down her throat. 'Mmm…mmm… mmm.'

She laughed as he gave her a gleaming, wickedly seductive look, and then she gave in to temptation and finished off the delicious fruit. It was a delightful medley of white and black grapes, orange, pineapple, pear and apple. 'That was exquisite,' she said.

'I'm glad you liked it.' His mouth curved. 'It was worth it, just to see the expression on your face.'

He started to clear away the dishes and murmured, 'Call Caitlin. I'll make coffee.'

She did as he suggested, keying in Caitlin's number, but even though she let it ring for a while, there was no answer. Frowning, she rang the house where Caitlin was supposed to be staying and waited for a response.

'I was just about to ring you,' Gemma's mother answered. 'We've been expecting her for the last half-hour or so, but she still hasn't arrived.'

They spoke for a minute or two more before Saskia finally cut the call.

'What is it?' Tyler asked. He looked concerned.

'She hasn't arrived at her friend's house,' she told him, fear rising in her throat. 'I must go and look for her. I can't think what might have happened. It was only a ten-minute ride by bus.' She stood up and started to look around for her bag. 'I have to go.'

'Wait for a moment. There's no need to panic.' Tyler came over to her and held her, wrapping his arms around her when she would have run from the house. 'Let's take a minute or two to think this through.'

'But she… Anything could have happened. She might have had an accident. She could have been abducted...' Her voice became frantic with worry.

'That's not likely in this small community. Calm down and we'll decide what we need to do.'

He'd said 'we'll decide' and that was what eventually made her stop wanting to rush out into the street. That and the warm pressure of his arms encircling her, soothing her and letting her know she wasn't alone.

'I must go after her.'

'We will. Let's assume she caught the bus, shall we? I'll drive us to the stop where she would have got off the bus, and we'll retrace her footsteps from there.'

'Yes, okay.'

He held her for a second or two longer and she laid her hand on his chest, reassured by the strong, steady beating of his heart. 'Thanks,' she said. 'Thanks for being here for me.'

He brushed her forehead with a gentle kiss. 'We'll find her.'

She nodded. 'Yes.' It was just intended as a

comforting gesture, that kiss, wasn't it? But she could still feel the warm imprint of it on her skin and, whether it meant anything or not, she had already taken it into her heart.

CHAPTER SEVEN

TYLER DROVE TOWARDS the east side of the island, following the route that the bus would
have taken. Darkness had fallen some time
ago, making it difficult to see anything very
clearly, but Saskia looked out of the car windows anyway, desperately searching for any
sign of Caitlin.

Soon they left the town behind them and
began to cross wild heathland as they approached the coastal area. Some half a mile
further on, when the road petered out at the bus
terminus where Caitlin would have been set
down, Tyler drew the car to a halt. They set off
to walk the rest of the way to Gemma's house.

'How far is it from here to the farmhouse?'
Tyler asked. 'I'm assuming she would have followed the footpath.'

'It's about a ten-minute walk, I think. I feel so awful now for letting her come out here alone, but she's been here before and never had any problems and I felt sure it would be all right.' Her voice shook as she thought about what might have happened and she took a deep breath to calm herself. 'We need to follow the path towards the coast.'

From here they could already see the craggy outline of the cove up ahead. Moonlight shimmered on the water and silhouetted the sand dunes where marram grass blew this way and that in the wind that came in off the sea.

Saskia shivered a little. She had put on a thin jacket but it wasn't too effective against the evening breeze that had sprung up. 'Here, let me keep you warm,' Tyler said, putting an arm around her and drawing her against the warmth of his body.

His thoughtfulness cheered her. Having him hold her like this helped to take some of the chill from around her heart. He was warm and supportive and everything she needed just then.

It was hard to believe that such a pleasurable evening could change so fast and turn into this awful nightmare.

They walked slowly, taking care to look all around them, searching for Caitlin in the bracken and among the hedgerows and all the while calling out her name.

'She wouldn't have run away, would she?' All kinds of dreadful scenarios were running through Saskia's head. 'I know she was unhappy, but I put it down to teenage angst, on top of everything else.' She couldn't conceal her anguish. 'I should have spent more time with her, tried to get her to talk to me a bit more.'

'Stop beating yourself up about it,' Tyler said. 'You did your best. And if she *was* trying to run away, where would she go? There's no ferry to get her to the mainland at this time of night.'

'No, I suppose you're right.'

They walked on, stopping every now and again to examine the hedgerows on either side, calling for Caitlin as they went. Saskia strained to distinguish the night sounds—the occasional hoot of an owl, the rustle of a shrew or a hedgehog scuffling through the undergrowth. But then, a few minutes later, there was another sound, a faint rasp, a murmuring of some sort.

'Wait…what was that?' She stood still, suddenly on alert. 'I think I heard something.'

There was only silence, though, and she called again. 'Caitlin, where are you?'

'Saskia…' It was very faint, a whisper almost, but she felt her heart begin to thud heavily.

'Did you hear that?'

Tyler nodded. 'I did. I think it came from over there, by the verge.' He pointed to where a hawthorn spread its branches, dipping low to the ground. There was a ditch covered in brushwood, filled with tangled undergrowth.

The low moaning sound came again. 'Sass…'

Through the darkness Saskia could barely make out a shadowy figure curled up on a bed of grass and leaves. The buckle of a belt shone dimly in the light of the moon, and elsewhere there was the faint gleam of a jewelled hair slide.

'Caitlin—thank heaven we've found you...' She moved forward to get closer to her, but her foot caught in the spreading roots of a gnarled tree and she gave a small moan of frustration as she struggled to release herself. 'Tyler, can you get to her?'

'Yes, it's all right, I have her.' Tyler clambered into the ditch and knelt down beside Caitlin. He carefully slid his hand under her head. 'Are you hurt?' he asked quietly. 'Can you tell us what happened?'

'I felt a bit dizzy...' Her voice was barely audible and she seemed to be having trouble thinking clearly. 'I must have fallen.' She closed her eyes, exhausted by the effort, and mumbled, 'My head hurts...and my ankle.'

'It's okay, Caitlin. You'll be all right now. I'll just quickly check you over and then we'll get you out of here.'

'Gemma—she'll be... I need to...'

By now Saskia had freed herself from the undergrowth and came to crouch down beside her niece. She held the girl's hand in hers, shocked by how cold it felt, as she soothed her and tried to ease her fears. 'I'll phone Gemma and let her know what happened. You don't need to worry about anything. We'll take care of whatever needs to be done.'

Tyler finished his examination. 'I don't think anything's broken,' he said, 'but I can't be sure about the ankle until we get her to the hospital. There has to be a reason for the dizziness, so we'd better be extra careful how we move her.'

Saskia nodded. 'Can we make a collar from my jacket? It's thin enough to fold.'

'Yes, we can try that.'

Saskia shrugged out of her jacket and rolled it into the shape of a neck collar. 'It's very makeshift, but it'll do for now,' she said. 'We'll have to tie the ends as best we can.'

When they were satisfied the collar was in place, it was at long last time to get Caitlin out of the ditch. 'I'll hold her head still while you lift her,' Saskia said.

'Okay, here we go.'

He carried Caitlin to the car and when Saskia opened the car doors he gently lifted the girl into the back seat and made sure she was safely secured.

Shivering a little, Saskia slid into the seat beside her. 'She's so cold from lying out there. It's been chilly today and the ground was damp.'

'Yes. She's suffering from hypothermia, I expect, but it's all right, I'll get a blanket from the boot. We'll keep her as warm as we can. In the meantime...' He took off his jacket and laid it over the ghostly-pale child, before going to rummage in the boot of the car.

He came back shortly and replaced his jacket with a new-looking fleecy blanket that he tucked around Caitlin. Then he draped his jacket around Saskia. 'Here, wear this. We can't have you collapsing from the cold as well.'

'Thanks.' Gratefully, she snuggled into it. It was still warm from his body and smelled faintly of his subtle cologne. It was the next best thing to being up close to him and for a little while she gave in to the guilty pleasure of imagining herself in his arms. She was beginning to realise that was what she wanted more and more, to be with him. She needed to have him near.

At the hospital, Tyler made sure that they were able to stay with Caitlin while she was being assessed. The makeshift collar was carefully exchanged for a proper one that would keep her neck stable, and then the team concentrated on trying to get her temperature back to normal. They gave her a warmed, humidified air/oxygen mix to inhale and wrapped her in special heat-retaining blankets. It was probably going to be a slow process, but Caitlin had been lying in the cold, damp ditch for some time and she was chilled to the bone.

Jason Samuels, the registrar on duty, took charge of Caitlin's care. He was quiet at first, making sure they were keeping tabs on her vital signs, but as time passed he recognised that she was a little more able to understand what was going on.

'I'll give you something for the pain in your ankle,' he told her, 'and as soon as you've warmed up a bit we'll take you over to X-Ray. I don't think anything's broken, but it's as well to be sure.'

A nurse handed her a mug of drinking chocolate. 'This should warm you from the inside,' she said, and handed her some tablets to take along with it.

'Have you had trouble with dizziness before this?' Jason asked.

Caitlin hesitated before answering. She was still having some trouble getting her thoughts together. 'It's been happening for a while,' she admitted. 'On and off, ever since Mum and Dad's accident.'

Startled, Jason glanced at Saskia. 'It sounds as though there might be a connection.'

Saskia frowned. 'I thought it was just the once—I'd no idea you'd been having problems ever since then. Why didn't you tell me?'

Caitlin wriggled her shoulders. 'It wasn't too bad and I didn't want to make a fuss, not after what happened to Mum and Dad.' She huddled into her blankets. 'They've been so ill, and the dizziness was nothing really.'

'But you were in the car with them when it happened, weren't you?' Saskia was swamped with feelings of guilt for not investigating further. 'Did you feel a nasty jolt at the time?'

'Yes, but I was okay.' She looked thoroughly miserable. 'It was just…my head's been feeling a bit muzzy ever since then and I've been getting a ringing in my ears.' She sighed wearily. 'I thought it would go away. I've been feeling really irritable—I'm sorry I've been so bad-tempered, Sass. I didn't know what was wrong with me.'

'Sweetheart, I wish you'd told me.' Saskia gave her a gentle hug.

'I'm sorry. I didn't want to complain when Mum and Dad were so ill. I thought this is nothing compared to what they've been through.'

'I think we need to get an X-ray and maybe

a CT scan, to try to find out what's going on,' Jason said. 'It does sound as if you might be suffering from whiplash, but we'll have a look at the films to be sure.' He turned to Saskia. 'I'm thinking it might be a good idea to keep her here overnight for observation, as she collapsed—just as a precaution, really, as her blood pressure's quite low. And, of course, we need to get her temperature back up.'

'Yes, I think you're right.' Saskia glanced at Caitlin. 'I'll pop home and pick up a few bits for you—everything you had with you is wet from being in the ditch. I could do that while you go down to Radiology—would you be okay with that? I'll be as quick as I can.'

'Yes, that's all right,' Caitlin agreed, adding anxiously, 'But you'll stay with me when you come back, won't you?'

'Yes, of course I will.' Saskia smiled at her. 'Don't worry about anything. I want you to try and get some rest.'

Tyler waited with her while Caitlin was

wheeled away to X-Ray, and then they walked together back to the car park.

'I think she'll be all right,' Tyler murmured as he started the car. 'She's still a bit shivery, but I think we found her in time, before deep hypothermia set in. And if there'd been a lot of damage from the whiplash we would probably have seen more specific symptoms before this.'

'Yes, I expect you're right.' She sent him a quick look. 'I'm really glad you were with me when we went to look for her. It made me feel so much better, having you there.'

His gaze flickered over her. 'I wouldn't have let you go alone. I wanted to be with you.'

They arrived back at the house a few minutes later and Saskia slid out of the car, in a hurry to get into the house to sort out a few bits.

'I'll go and change into some clean clothes while you put a few things in a bag,' Tyler said as he walked her to her door. He made a rueful smile. 'After scrabbling around in a ditch and being caught up on thorns, I'm afraid these trousers are only fit for the dustbin.'

She made a face. 'I'm sorry about that. You looked great in them, too.'

He laughed. 'Really?' One dark brow quirked upwards. 'Well, that's good to know.' Instinctively, he moved closer to her, his hand moving as though he was going to slide it around her waist in a warm, intimate embrace...but at the last second he stopped, perhaps thinking better of it, and contented himself instead with sliding a hand down her arm in a light caress. 'I'm glad we managed to get some time together earlier,' he murmured. 'We should do it more often—but maybe without the drama next time.'

'I think you're right.' On impulse, she reached up and kissed him fleetingly on the mouth, her palms flattening on his chest. 'I don't know what I'd have done without you.'

She heard the breath catch in his throat. He seemed stunned by that kiss, momentarily pinned to the spot, motionless. But when he would have responded and tugged her into his arms she swiftly evaded him.

'I should get these things for Caitlin.' She didn't know what had come over her, what had possessed her to kiss him, and she was awkwardly conscious that she'd stepped over the invisible line he'd drawn. But she wanted him, needed him—and all her thoughts of steering clear of men and being afraid for the future had flown out of the window since she'd got to know Tyler. Was this love? It had to be— it was all-encompassing, it filled her up, took over her being, and she'd never felt this way before, never cared for any man so much.

'I won't be long,' she said. 'I promised Caitlin we'd be back at the hospital before she knew it. Let yourself in if you're ready before me—I don't always hear the doorbell if I'm upstairs.'

'Uh…yeah…okay.'

As landlord, he had his own key to the house, though he'd never presumed to use it. Was this yet another line she was crossing? Somehow, after the events of the evening, it didn't seem to matter any more.

She went into the house and dashed upstairs.

Caitlin was usually fussy about what she wore, but Saskia gathered up a fresh outfit of skirt, leggings and a warm top for the morning, in the hope that the teenager would be well enough to come home by then. Of course, she would need pyjamas and set of underwear along with a toothbrush and comb, and Saskia quickly added these to an overnight bag.

Then she went into the bathroom and freshened up, changing into a clean pair of jeans and a different pair of shoes. She added a light touch of make-up and after looking around to make sure she'd not forgotten anything she went back down the stairs.

The doorbell rang and she smiled faintly. Did this mean Tyler didn't feel right about letting himself in? Perhaps she'd been presuming too much.

She opened the door, ready to greet him and show him that she had everything in hand. They could leave right away.

Only it wasn't Tyler who was standing there,

and the smile faded from her lips, her heart tripping in an uncomfortable, jerky beat.

'Hi,' Michael said. 'I've been waiting around for ages, hoping you would come home.'

She stared at him, nonplussed. 'Michael, what are you doing here? How did you find out where I was living?'

'You phoned me, remember? It was fairly easy to find you after that.' He studied her, a slight smile playing around his mouth. 'Aren't you going to ask me in?'

'I can't,' she said. 'I have to go out—to the hospital. I can't stay here.'

'Just for a minute or two? I won't keep you. I just wanted to say I'm sorry if I've been making life difficult for you. At first, when you were still working with me, it's true, I wanted to punish you, but after you left…well, I suppose I thought if you had nowhere else to go you would come back to me…back to your old job.'

Reluctantly, she stepped back to let him in. As soon as Tyler arrived they would leave, and maybe this would be her one last chance to show Michael that things were well and truly over between them.

'I only phoned you to find out why you were implying that I'd made mistakes with my patients,' she said. 'I didn't mean to give you the impression that I wanted us to get together again. I'm sorry if you got the wrong idea.'

'I know. I do understand.' He walked with her to the kitchen. 'I don't blame you for breaking things off—I was difficult to get along with, I know. But I hated it when you left. I always hoped—'

'I'm not coming back, Michael,' she said. 'I thought I made that clear to you.'

'Yes, you did.' He ran a hand through his dark hair. 'But I want you to know that I can change. I could be everything you want...' He came towards her and she kept moving backwards until she came up against the hard rim of the worktop.

'No,' she told him. 'It isn't going to happen.'

'But if you would just let me show you...' By

now he was so close that he was almost touching her and she felt stifled. She didn't want to make a scene, but things might easily get out of hand.

'She said it isn't going to happen.' Tyler's voice cut in, breaking through the tension in the room. 'I'm afraid you've had a wasted journey, Michael. You should go back to wherever it is that you're staying tonight and then head out on the ferry in the morning. There's no point in you hanging around here any longer.' Instinctively, Saskia edged sideways, trying to get closer to him.

Michael's eyes widened as he looked from Tyler to Saskia and back again. 'You and she—? Are you...?' He couldn't bring himself to say the words.

'That's right.' Tyler looked him straight in the eye and, watching him, Saskia felt her jaw drop. He'd implied they were together, a couple. Conscious of Michael's scrutiny, she quickly tried to pull herself together. 'So, you see,' Tyler went on, 'you need to believe what

Saskia's been telling you. It's over between you two. It's finished.'

Michael crumpled as though he'd received a blow to the stomach, and much as she wanted him to get the message Saskia hated to see him suffering like this.

'I'm sorry, Michael,' she said. 'It's just that you and I were never really suited, and this was bound to happen some time.' She studied him thoughtfully, with some sympathy. 'You know, there are lots of women out there who would love to be with you. You're a good-looking man, you do a great job—you're a caring, wonderful doctor. You have everything going for you. All you need to do is put this behind you and move on.'

'I didn't know,' he said. He turned away and began to walk a little unsteadily back along the hallway. Saskia followed him. 'I never dreamt...' He looked as though he was in a state of shock.

Tyler came to stand by the door. 'Are you safe to drive? Where are you staying?'

'I'm booked in at The Schooner.' He sent Saskia a piercing glance. 'I'll be there until after breakfast tomorrow morning if you want to talk to me again.'

'I don't think so,' she said. 'I'm sorry, Michael. Goodbye.'

They watched him drive away and then she turned to Tyler. 'You let him believe we were a couple,' she said. Her green eyes were clear and bright as she looked at him. She wanted so much for it to be true. But had he made it up to persuade Michael to leave, or could it be there was a germ of truth hidden behind the statement? She longed for him to say he wanted them to be together.

Instead, he hesitated, turning away from her so that his features were shadowed. He shrugged.

'It was a white lie. There didn't seem to be any other way he would get the message.' He gave her a quick, searching glance as she struggled to hide her disappointment. 'Why, does it bother you?'

She shook her head. 'Not really.' She desperately searched for a way out of the situation, to come up with a reason for her reaction. 'If he starts to tell people that we're an item, sooner or later it will get back to everyone at the hospital. How will you feel then?'

His mouth made a crooked shape. 'I doubt anyone will believe it. They all have me hooked up with Imogen.'

She stared at him. 'Imogen?' Pain lanced through her. She'd vaguely suspected something like this, that he and Imogen had something going between them, but was he really admitting it?

But if that was the case, why had he kissed her the other day? Had it only been meant as a comforting gesture after all, something that had quickly got out of hand?

She'd been growing more and more close to Tyler, but it looked as though the feelings and emotions were all on her side, not his.

'It's natural enough, don't you think? Imogen and I are very much alike, and we work well together. Why wouldn't we be a couple?'

'But…' She was staggered by what he was saying, struggling to take it in. 'You work with her—doesn't that go against your principles? After you kissed me you told me it wasn't right because you were my boss.'

He made a wry smile, but his head went back a fraction and she sensed his hesitation. 'I don't pretend to be perfect. Maybe I was caught unawares and my self-control slipped. After all, I'm as vulnerable as the next man when it comes to being with a beautiful, sexy woman who needs help. But…' his mouth flattened '…when all's said and done, I meant what I said. It wouldn't be right to take advantage of you when you're here on a three-month trial.'

'And nothing could come of it anyway…isn't that right?' She shot him a bleak, challenging glance. 'We're opposites, aren't we? My life's pretty much a shambles, and I'm living from day to day, hoping to get by, whereas you have everything mapped out. You're at the peak of your career, you have a lovely house where everything has its place, and all you need is the ideal woman to share it with you...someone who would keep it in immaculate condition.'

She frowned. 'I suppose Imogen fits the bill perfectly.' It was a sour comment, and she regretted it as soon as she'd made it.

'We should go to the hospital,' she said, exasperated with herself. 'Forget what I said. It's been a long day and I guess I'm out of sorts.'

He sent her a long, brooding look, but he didn't say anything. Instead, he picked up Caitlin's bag and led the way out of the house.

CHAPTER EIGHT

'HOW IS SHE? What do the scans show?' Saskia hurried into A and E with Tyler, anxious to hear any news of Caitlin.

For now she had no choice but to put any problems she had with Tyler to one side. She couldn't help how she felt about him…she loved him and couldn't bear to think of him not being in her life…but was it possible that he didn't return those feelings? Had she been misreading the signals he'd been giving out? She was convinced he wanted her, and at the same time he had struggled to draw back from her—was it really so important to him that he didn't confuse his role as mentor with his feelings for her? Or was it really Imogen who lay at the root of him holding back?

Jason put the films up on screen for her and

Tyler to see. 'It looks as though the muscles and ligaments in Caitlin's neck have been strained, which, of course, makes them inflamed, painful and obviously tender. It'll probably take a couple of months or so before they're back to normal.' He glanced at Saskia. 'She's lucky in that the facet joints and the discs seem to be okay.'

Saskia gave a sigh of relief. 'And the dizziness…do we know what's causing that?'

He shook his head. 'It's possible that there was some sort of minor injury to the inner ear—to the balance centre. That, too, should eventually right itself.'

'So what's the procedure now—anti-inflammatories?'

'Yes, I've started her on them and we'll prescribe them for when she leaves hospital. We can fix her up with a soft collar, too, if she'd like to wear one. If she finds it helps, that's all well and good. If she still has problems after a week or two I could try her with muscle relaxants.'

'Massage therapy might help,' Tyler put in. 'It would increase the blood flow to the region and help with healing.'

Jason nodded. 'It's worth a try.'

'Thanks for everything you've done,' Saskia said. 'I'll go and sit with her, though I expect what she needs most of all is sleep.'

Tyler shot her a quick glance. 'Would you like me to stay with you?'

She hesitated. More than anything, she wanted to say yes, but he'd already done enough and it wouldn't be fair to keep him waiting around any longer, would it? None of this was his problem. She shook her head. 'No, that's all right. We'll be fine. But thanks for bringing me back here. I really appreciate it.'

'That's okay. Give me a call tomorrow when you're ready to leave and I'll come and pick you up.'

'Uh…thanks.' She doubted that she would call him. It was one thing to accept his help when she thought he cared for her, but quite another if he was just along for the ride. She'd try to get home by any other means if possible.

He gave her an oddly puzzled look and she wondered if there was something in her tone or her expression that had given her thoughts away.

He turned, though, and she watched him walk away before going over to the observation ward to sit by Caitlin's bedside. She felt totally alone and empty inside.

A glance at the monitor showed her that Caitlin's blood pressure was still low and her pulse was slow. 'How are you feeling?' she asked her. 'Are you a bit warmer now?'

'Yes, thanks. As soon as my temperature was up enough I persuaded them to let me have a warm bath—they made the room all hot and steamy—and all I want now are my own pyjamas. I hate this cotton, backless thing they've given me to wear and this stripy hospital dressing gown.'

'Oh, well, that's soon remedied.' Saskia smiled and unzipped the holdall she'd brought with her. 'I brought your favourite pjs and your bathrobe. Do you want some help to put them on?'

'Yes, please. My neck and shoulders are a bit stiff. In fact, I'm achy all over.'

'I expect it'll take a while before you're back to your usual self,' Saskia said, as she helped Caitlin put on her pyjamas. 'Have you had any more dizziness?'

'Just a bit, but I'm okay.'

'Hmm. I expect a good night's sleep will help. Close your eyes if you want, and try to get some rest. I'll be here right next to you.'

Caitlin looked relieved. 'I think I will, if you don't mind.'

Saskia gave her a hug and settled back in her chair. At some point in the night she, too, dozed off, but she woke up in the morning when the nurse came along to check Caitlin's blood pressure.

'Oh, that's a lot better,' the nurse said with a smile. 'We'll see if she can manage to eat some breakfast and then Dr Samuels will be along to see at her.'

Caitlin sat up in bed and rubbed her eyes. 'Do you think I'll be able to go home today?' she asked Saskia.

'Perhaps a bit later on, if you're feeling all right.' She looked at her niece carefully. There was certainly more colour in her cheeks now.

It was a couple of hours into the afternoon, though, before Jason decided she was well enough to be discharged. They had to wait for the hospital pharmacy to dispense Caitlin's medication before they could leave, but it gave Saskia an opportunity to pack the teenager's belongings into the holdall and make sure she didn't leave anything behind.

'Hi, there. Are you girls ready to go home?'

Saskia's heart skipped a beat as she looked up and saw Tyler walking into the observation ward. He was dressed in casual clothes, dark trousers and an open-necked shirt, and he looked terrific.

'What are you doing here?' she asked, looking at him in surprise. 'I wasn't expecting you.'

'I asked Jason to keep me informed of what was going on,' he said. 'I had the feeling you might be foolish enough to pay for a taxi—I was pretty sure you wouldn't decide to walk home with Caitlin just out of hospital.'

A flush of pink stole across her cheeks. 'Well, you've done so much for us already. I didn't want to put you to any more trouble.'

'If I didn't want to do it, I'd tell you.' He picked up the holdall. 'The medication's ready for you at the nurses' station,' he told Caitlin, 'so we can leave as soon as you're ready.'

Caitlin glanced at him. She didn't say anything, but she smiled and dropped into step beside him, accepting the help of a supporting arm from Saskia.

It was only later, when they were back home and Tyler had gone back to his own house to catch up on some research he was doing, that she looked at Saskia and said, 'I think he has a thing for you.'

Saskia shook her head. 'No, I don't think so. There's someone at work who's much more his type.'

Caitlin frowned. 'He can't be that serious about her. He's always looking at you—he can't take his eyes off you. He just doesn't want you to know it, for some reason.'

Saskia smiled and tried to make light of it, but Caitlin had certainly given her something to think about. Why would he not want her to know how he felt about her? Was it really the three-month trial that was making him keep her at arm's length? And how had she managed to get herself so hot and bothered about him when she knew she should have been doing her best to stay away from him? It was all very confusing.

Deep down, though, she knew the answer. It was impossible for her *not* to care for him. Somehow he'd worked his way into her heart and now she couldn't contemplate life without him. Was she being irrational? Would it all end in tears and recriminations, the way it had with Michael?

Tyler was different, though, she felt sure. He would never be mean or deliberately hurtful, or react in the way that Michael had done, would he?

At the hospital, over the next week, they both tried to keep things between them on a professional footing. They managed to forge a reasonable, if somewhat tense way of going on together. It was as though neither of them dared relax their guard.

'I need to go and see a patient on the way home from work,' he told her a short time before their shift was due to end on Friday. 'It's as a favour for a friend who's a bit worried about her son.'

'Okay.' They'd both had a difficult, busy day, so she guessed this must be important to him.

'She lives in the opposite direction from us, but I could drop you off at home and then double back, if it's going to be a problem for you.'

She shook her head. 'No, it's all right. You don't want to have to do that.' He'd had a particularly fraught day, dealing with one emergency after another, so he could probably do without the extra burden. 'The children will be at Rosie's house after school. I can ring her and tell her I'll be a little late picking them up. I'm sure she won't mind.'

'Good. Thanks. That will save me some time—I've quite a lot on this weekend with this hospital administrators' meeting coming up, so time's precious.'

'Oh... I heard about that—it's scheduled for tomorrow afternoon, isn't it? Aren't you going to be one of the speakers—at the hospital in Truro? Noah said you'd been working on it with Imogen this last day or so—something to do with reorganising cardiovascular facilities for the region.' She didn't want to think about how unsettling that had been, knowing that he and Imogen were closeted together in his office for long stretches of time. 'He said something about a presentation.'

'That's right. I was called in at the last minute when someone had to drop out, so I have to spend the next few hours working on my speech. I need things to run as smoothly as possible if I'm to get it finished in time.'

She nodded. 'You could have done without this callout, I expect. Have you any idea what's wrong with your friend's son?'

He frowned. 'I don't think it's anything too serious—at least, I hope it isn't. He's been having some headaches these last few months. Apparently he's suffering a particularly bad one today and she's concerned about him.'

'Hmm.' She thought about it. 'I know it sounds odd, but perhaps it's something to do with the weather—it's been quite hot and humid these last few days and some forecasters are predicting a storm. It's surprising, but a lot of people get headaches in those conditions. It's all due to hot air sweeping across the Atlantic from the Azores, or something along those lines.'

'That's your candid opinion?' Amusement

glinted in his blue eyes. 'I can't see that going down too well if I start basing my diagnoses on the vagaries of the weather, can you? We'd probably do better if we stick to looking at actual symptoms and work our way back from there, don't you think?'

'Yeah, well…I was just saying…' She broke off, seeing his shoulders moving with suppressed laughter, and she aimed a mock thump at his arm. 'Stop making fun of me. I'm right, I know I am—I've read about it.'

'Yeah…yeah…if you say so.'

A short time later they drove along the main highway to his friend's house. 'I know Nicole and her husband through my sister,' he explained. 'We've known each other since we were teenagers.'

As soon as they arrived at Nicole's address Tyler introduced Saskia and they were shown into the sitting room where a boy aged around ten was lying curled up in a foetal position on the sofa. He was covering his eyes with his hands.

'Thanks for coming,' his mother said quietly. 'He's been like this for the last couple of hours. He's been sick quite a bit and complaining of the light, and any kind of noise upsets him and seems to make things worse.'

Tyler went to sit on the edge of the settee. 'Hi, Lewis. Would it be all right if I take a look at you? Perhaps we'll be able to do something about this headache of yours.'

Lewis slowly drew himself up into a sitting position. It was plain to see that he was completely incapacitated by the headache. He looked drowsy, utterly exhausted, and there were dark circles under his eyes. Beads of sweat had broken out on his forehead. 'Can you make it go away?' he pleaded.

'I'm sure we can. Do you want to tell me about it? When did it start?'

'This afternoon, at school. I kept seeing all these sparkly lights in my eyes and one of the teachers had to bring me home.'

Gently, Tyler examined him, checking his

reflexes and paying particular attention to his ears, throat and glands.

'First of all,' he said when he had finished, 'you need to know that nothing dangerous is going on here. It's just a very nasty headache that can be treated.'

Nicole relaxed her shoulders and gave a soft sigh of relief. 'It's not like an ordinary headache, though, is it?' she said.

'No, that's right…it's a migraine. They're usually brought on by some kind of trigger—fluorescent light, flickering lights, certain foods or smells, stress, tiredness…even changes in the weather can do it in some circumstances.' He sent Saskia a quick glance and she gave him a superior, *I told you so* look in return. 'What you need to do,' he added, 'is find Lewis's particular trigger and get him to avoid it as best he can. It will help if you keep a diary to note down the circumstances around when the headaches start.'

He opened his medical case and drew out a packet of tablets. 'He should take one of these now—if he doesn't manage to keep it down I can give him an injection, but this should help with the sickness and the headache. I'll write you out a prescription for some more tablets, and he'll need to take one of them at the first sign of a migraine. The sooner he takes it, the better it will work.'

'Thanks, Tyler. I know I shouldn't have bothered you, but I couldn't get an urgent appointment with the family doctor and I was so worried. I knew you wouldn't let me down.'

'That's all right. I'll send a letter to his GP and he'll follow up on his treatment from here on.'

They waited with Lewis for a while to make sure he kept the medication down, and it was only when the boy finally fell asleep that Tyler made a move to leave. 'I'm sure he'll be okay now,' he said, 'but if you're worried at all, give me a call.'

They said goodbye and left the house. It was getting dark outside and around them the trees were billowing, their branches bending in the wind.

Saskia slid into the passenger seat of the car. 'The sky looks heavy with cloud,' she said, adding, tongue in cheek, 'You know, I might already have mentioned it, but I think we've been through a low-pressure system lately and we're definitely in for one of those storms that builds up over the Atlantic.'

Tyler grinned and turned the car off the main road, heading for home. 'Okay, okay...I get the point.'

They picked up the children from Rosie and then Saskia shepherded them into their house as thunder grumbled overhead and the first rain began to fall. Tyler parked the car in the garage and cast a quick glance at the sky before hurrying next door.

The storm continued to rumble for the next hour or so while Saskia went about her chores, and she was baking Cornish pasties when the lights suddenly went out. She stood in darkness for a while, trying to work out what to do for the best. There was a lantern somewhere around and a couple of torches in one of the kitchen drawers, but it was difficult to find her way about until her eyes grew accustomed to the dark.

'What's happened?' Becky asked.

'The electricity's gone off,' Caitlin answered.

'It's because of the storm, isn't it?'

'Yes,' Saskia agreed, as she felt her way around the kitchen to the drawer she needed. 'I expect the power lines are down. We'll just have to do the best we can for now. Try to stay where you are,' she told the children. 'We don't want you bumping into things.'

A flash of lightning lit the room and everyone stared, caught like rabbits in headlights. Charlie's bottom lip quivered and Boomer looked up from his bed in the corner of the room briefly, before going back to sleep.

'It's all right, Charlie,' Saskia murmured, pulling open the drawer and feeling inside it for one of the torches. 'There's nothing to worry about. It just means we don't have any lights or any means of cooking until the engineers get the power back on.' The Aga was powered totally by electricity and, of course, they would have no means of heating.

'Won't we get any dinner?' Charlie asked fretfully in the darkness. 'I'm hungry.'

'Um—I think the pasties are just about cooked. I'll leave them in the hot oven for a while to finish off.' She found the torch and switched it on. 'Becky, you can hold the other one. Caitlin, you need to sit down. We don't want you getting dizzy in the dark.'

The doorbell rang some fifteen minutes later and she went to answer it, guided by the beam of the torch.

'I wondered how you're managing with the power cut?' Tyler was holding a lantern that burned brightly in the darkness. Rain lashed at him, and she quickly drew him inside the house. 'Do you have enough candles or lamps?' he asked.

She shook her head. 'It didn't occur to me to get any in,' she said, biting her lip at her lack of foresight. 'We're all in the kitchen, sitting round the table by torchlight.' She made a wry smile. 'The children are bored to tears already because they can't get Wi-Fi.'

His mouth curved briefly. 'Well, luckily I have plenty of battery-powered lamps and a duel-fuel Aga, so at least I can boil a pan of water for hot drinks and one of the ovens is working.' His brow creased. 'Why don't you all come round to my house while the power's out? If the lines are down it could take quite a while to get the lights back on—last time this happened it was several hours before things were back to normal.'

'Okay…if you're sure?' It sounded as though they might be in this for the long haul, and although she was certain she would be able to cope, she doubted the children would manage for long. 'Would it be all right if the children bring some toys with them? And what about Boomer?'

'Yes, that's fine…and, of course, Boomer must come.' He moved restlessly. 'Get them to bring whatever they need. The only thing is, I'm afraid you'll have to excuse me while I get on with my presentation—I printed out what I'd done of the speech because I was worried the power might go off, but I still have to make alterations to it and sort out the slide presentation while the battery power lasts on the laptop.'

'Of course. I understand.' She glanced at him. He'd taken the time to think about how they were getting along, but he seemed tense, in a hurry to get on, and she was concerned for him. He'd missed lunch at work today because of an emergency that had come in, and she suspected he was driving himself way too hard.

He handed her the lantern. 'Take this with you while you find what they need. I'll manage with the torch.'

'Thanks, Tyler.'

They quickly gathered together whatever they thought they might need, and finally Saskia took the pasties from the oven and put them all in a large ovenproof dish with a lid to keep the heat in. At least they wouldn't go hungry.

A few minutes later they all hurried over to Tyler's house, keeping their heads down because of the driving rain and clutching their coats around them to keep out the fierce wind. Another flash of lightning cracked across the sky, and a few seconds later thunder rumbled ominously overhead.

'I don't like it,' Charlie said, pinned to the spot, his face crumpling, and Tyler swooped him up into his arms and carried him into the house.

'It's fine. It's nothing to worry about,' he told him. 'If you count how many seconds pass between the lightning flash and the thunder, you can tell how far away the lightning is. Try it next time. Every five seconds is about one mile, so I reckon the lightning's about two miles away.' He looked at Charlie, but the boy had his head buried in his jacket. 'Anyway, it's not going to hurt you.'

Once they were all inside the house, Tyler

made sure they were comfortable and settled in the living room before he excused himself to go back to work in his study. 'Do you think you have enough light in here?' he asked Saskia. 'I can bring in some more lamps if you need them.'

'No, we're fine,' she said. She looked around. 'They've already sorted themselves out…see?' Becky and Charlie had tipped a tub of small plastic building blocks over the large Oriental rug and were busy building a castle of some sort, and Caitlin was cosy in an armchair, listening to music through her earphones.

'And you—what will you do? Will you be all right? I hate to leave you like this, but I need to get this presentation sorted. I have to be on my way to the mainland by ten in the morning.'

'I've brought a book with me,' she said. 'I should be able to read it well enough with the light from the lamp.' He'd placed an oil-burning lamp on the table by the sofa. 'Don't worry about us. We'll be okay.'

'All right, then. Make yourselves hot drinks

and snacks whenever you want them. You'll find everything you need in the cupboards in the kitchen.'

'Thanks.' She sent him a quick glance. 'Have you eaten yet? I know you didn't have time for lunch.'

'I grabbed something from the snack bar this afternoon,' he said. 'I'm fine.'

'Hmm. What was that—a sticky bun?' She knew she'd guessed right from the crooked slant of his mouth. She didn't think he was fine at all. It wasn't like him to appear pressured in any way, but his features were taut and from the way his silky black hair peaked in small spikes she guessed he'd been running his hand through it.

He escaped to the study, leaving Saskia to make her way to the kitchen, where she set about serving up the hot pasties. The appetising smell soon wafted on the air. The combination of beef, onion and potato in a thick pastry crust should make for a warming, filling meal, and would keep everyone happy for a while.

When the children were settled around the table, tucking in, she made a pot of tea and slid a couple of pasties on a plate for Tyler.

She knocked on the door of his study and went in. 'I thought you might like something to eat,' she said.

He looked up at her, frowning. 'I can't take food from you,' he protested. 'You'll have made enough for yourself and the children. I'll get something later when I've finished working.'

She shook her head. 'We've all eaten—I made plenty because I never know who's going to want more. Please, eat up. I made you some tea as well.'

He made as though to prevaricate and she said firmly, 'You have to get some food inside you or you won't be in any fit state to do anything. You're a doctor—I shouldn't have to tell you that.'

He smiled and gave in, pushing away his paperwork and accepting the plate she offered. 'Mmm...these are good,' he said, biting into a golden pasty and savouring the moment. 'Perfect.'

'I'm glad you think so.' She glanced at the piles of paper on his desk and the colourful diagram that was displayed on the laptop screen. 'How's it going?'

'All right, I think. I'm trying to get as much done as I can while the battery lasts. I have to change the order of some of the points in the speech and edit some of the slides, but I'm getting there.' He took another bite from his pasty.

'Good, I'm glad. But perhaps the power will come back on soon and you won't need to worry.'

'Actually, this is going to last for quite a while,' he said. 'I rang the electricity company and they say the lines are down and it could take several hours before the problem's fixed. It might even be as late as tomorrow morning.'

He gave it some thought. 'Perhaps you should sort out some nightwear for yourself and the children if you're going to stay here overnight. Caitlin and Becky can have the large guest bedroom, and Charlie should be okay in the room next to them.' He glanced at her. 'There's a second en suite room that you could use.'

'Oh...' She was startled. 'I hadn't expected it would come to that. It's thoughtful of you to offer. Thank you.'

'You're welcome.' He swallowed some of the hot tea and then gave her a searching glance. 'So, how are things going with you lately? Is there any more news about your brother and his wife?'

'Megan seems to be feeling much better now, but Sam...' she sent him a troubled look '...Sam is having some problems with his breathing. They're not sure what's causing it. It's not the infection any longer because that cleared up.'

'I'm sorry. It's a worry for you.'

'Yes.'

'You've had a lot to deal with. And what about that business last weekend? Have you heard any more from Michael? I take it he went back to Cornwall without giving you any more trouble?'

'He did.' She sat down on the edge of his desk and his gaze followed her movements, gliding over the neat fit of her skinny jeans and lingering on the floaty, scoop-necked top that she was wearing. 'Uh…he rang me a couple of days ago to say that he was sorry for the way he'd behaved over the last few months. He said he'd come to his senses and that I could have my old job back any time I wanted. He said he wouldn't give me any trouble.'

His eyes narrowed a fraction. 'How do you feel about that?'

She hesitated. 'I'm not sure. I think I trust him not to cause problems for me any more— he said he acted the way he did because he'd become obsessed with me and he wanted me back. He thought if I didn't have a job here I would end up going back to him. It's a sort of twisted logic—but he seems to be aware of his behaviour and wants to change.'

She sighed. 'I suppose talking things through

with him made me take stock of my situation. If things don't work out for me here, getting my old job back might seriously be an option after all.'

His brows shot up in astonishment. 'You wouldn't really consider going back there, would you?'

She gave a small shrug. 'I might not have any choice—after all, I don't have any guarantee of a job here, do I? I'd have to look for work—not necessarily at my old hospital but somewhere on the mainland.'

Guardedly, he stood up. 'I wouldn't have thought there was going to be a problem over you working here. After all, you only have to get through the next few weeks—'

'Maybe, but how do I know that at the end of it you won't decide I'm not up to the job? What if another patient decides to go walkabout or someone's medication doesn't do what it's supposed to do? Or if my seasickness becomes a problem?'

She looked at him, her green eyes troubled.

'After all, you're the one who had doubts about me in the first place—you're the one who set up the three-month trial condition, aren't you? Under any other circumstances, with a different employer, I would have been given the job outright. It was only because Michael planted the seed of doubt in your mind that you thought I might one day let you down.'

She frowned. 'I've been on edge ever since I started work here. I'm not sure I want to go on feeling that I'm somehow not up to scratch and have to go on proving myself.'

'You don't have to prove yourself and you shouldn't feel that way. You're a good doctor, Saskia. I'm sorry if I made you feel otherwise.' He ran his hand lightly down her arm. 'You're right, I was concerned in the beginning, but I was wrong. I realise that now. But I can't change the contract terms—James Gregson is a stickler for following procedure. It isn't too long to wait, is it? I don't want you to leave… you must know that.'

He was thoroughly shaken by what she'd

said, that was plain to see, but the truth was she didn't feel secure, and she didn't know how he truly felt about her. 'Perhaps. I'm not really sure. I don't always understand where you're coming from. I think I'm getting mixed signals from you, Tyler. It's confusing. I don't know where I am.'

'I think you're a great doctor and a wonderful, caring woman...' His blue gaze searched her face. 'I hate to think of you leaving. All I know is I can't bear the thought of you going back to him. I need you to stay here, Saskia... with me.' His hand slid around her waist and came to rest, palm flat, against the small of her back. 'I need you. I can't stop thinking about you. You're beautiful, irresistible...you take my breath away.'

He drew her up against him, pressuring her against his long, hard body, and before she knew what was happening his head bent towards her and he was kissing her, an urgent, passionate kiss full of pent-up emotion. She felt the taut strength of his body next to hers, his powerful thighs compelling her into the rounded edge of the mahogany desk, and all the while his arms enclosed her, his hands stroking her soft curves.

'I've tried to hold back all this time,' he said huskily, 'but it's been nothing but torment.' His hands swept along the length of her and came to linger on the firm swell of her hips. 'You can't really be thinking of going back to him, can you?'

'Not to him…I never said that…but…' Her voice trailed away as his hands moved over her, seeking out all the contours of her body. He lightly cupped her breast, his thumb brushing the hardening nub in slow, mesmerising circles. 'Tyler, I…'

He stopped her words with tender kisses over her mouth, her cheeks, gliding along the column of her throat in a sensual, exhilarating journey of exploration. 'I can't bear to think of him sweet-talking you into going back to him. I need you,' he said again, his voice rough with desire. 'I want you so much.'

She lifted her hands to his chest, feeling the warmth of his skin emanating from beneath his shirt. She let her fingers trail over the rigid six-pack of his stomach and upwards to explore the inviting, smooth silk of his pectorals. As her hands roamed a soft groan escaped him.

'It feels so good to have you touch me that way.'

She lifted her face for his kiss, lost herself in the wonder of being with him this way. But at the back of her mind she couldn't help wondering whether she was making a big mistake. Could she really be letting this happen?

She wanted him, loved being in his arms. She longed to have him tell her the things she wanted to hear, but how could that ever come about? He didn't love her, did he? He'd never said those words she desperately needed him to say. And through it all he was still her boss, the man who held power over her future. Hadn't she told herself she would never get into this situation ever again? What was wrong with her that she couldn't find the willpower to keep him at arm's length?

A piercing beep came from somewhere on the desk behind them, and for a moment she stayed perfectly still, unable to take it in. It wasn't the beep of a phone or any other sound that she recognised right away.

It came again, and Tyler stiffened. 'No...no... how could I have been so stupid?' He straightened and eased himself away from her.

'What is it?' She looked at him in confusion.

'The laptop—the battery's about to give up.' He grimaced. 'I need to sort this out; I've got to save my work before I lose what I've been doing for the last hour.'

He looked at her, his expression full of frustration, exasperation and apology.

'It's okay.' She stepped to one side so that he could sort out the problem. Perhaps it was just as well that they had been interrupted. She still wasn't clear in her head that she was doing the right thing. Hadn't Michael used soft words and easy charm to convince her that he was the right man for her? Wasn't she in danger of falling into that same old trap?

She left Tyler to work his magic with the computer, telling him briefly, 'If you need to go on working, you can use my laptop. You just need to save your work to a memory stick and transfer it over. I brought it with me.'

Distracted, he looked at her. 'Thanks. That would be great.'

She took her laptop to him then shut the study door and went to help the children get ready for bed.

She had to go next door to pick up what they needed, but she was back within a few minutes, glad of the light burning in Tyler's house and the warmth that emanated from the flickering flames of the gas fire in the lounge and the heat from the Aga in the kitchen.

Tyler was still working in the study when she decided to go to bed. It seemed that whatever he set out to do, he gave it everything he had. Wouldn't it be something if he decided he wanted her at all costs?

It wasn't long, though, before doubts began to creep back in. Hadn't he said that Imogen was the ideal woman for him? Perhaps not in so many words, but he'd said they were very much alike and asked why they wouldn't be a couple. So why was he kissing another woman? Had his kisses been born out of a momentary, compelling desire, or was there something more going on in his subconscious?

She didn't sleep well. The storm raged through the night and she tossed and turned as flashes of lightning lit up the room and thunder growled. In the early hours Charlie clambered into bed beside her, snuggling into the shelter of her arms.

He wasn't there when she woke in the morning. Sitting up in bed, she looked around, befuddled for a second or two until she had her bearings. The electric clock at the side of the bed still had a blank screen so obviously the power hadn't been restored overnight. That had been some storm.

Hurriedly, she washed and dressed, pulling

on a pair of blue jeans and a button-through top that clung to her curves and outlined her slender waist.

'Can we make breakfast?' Becky asked, coming into the room as she finished dressing. 'We're all hungry.'

'Yes, I should think so. I'll see what there is.'

'We had cereals first thing, but Charlie's starving and Caitlin says we have to wait till you come down before we help ourselves to anything else.'

'Well, she's right. This isn't our house.' She mulled it over. 'I'll have to do a grocery shop and stock up again for Tyler. Is he up and about yet?'

'I haven't seen him.'

'Okay, well, we'll go and see what we can rustle up, shall we? I expect he'll want something to eat before he leaves.'

'All right.'

Saskia's jaw dropped when walked into the once pristine kitchen a couple of minutes later. It was a mess. Whoever had set out the cereals for breakfast—Becky and Charlie, she suspected—had left small puddles of milk, sugar and wheat flakes all over the worktop. And that wasn't all…

'I gave Boomer wheat flakes for his breakfast,' Charlie said. 'He liked them. And then he wanted to go out, so I let him into the garden. I think it's a bit muddy out there after all the rain.'

'Yes, I can see that.' A trail of muddy paw prints ran higgledy-piggledy across the tiled floor.

'Good grief.' Tyler's voice sounded from behind her and she half turned to look at him. His eyes were wide with disbelief. His face was dark with overnight shadow, lending him a roguish, sexy air, and his hair was glistening as though he'd just come from the shower. 'How long have the children been up?'

'Um…about an hour, I think. They're used to being up and about early for school.'

He winced. 'Have you seen the state of the

lounge? It looks as if a bomb's gone off in there.'

'Uh…no, I haven't yet.' She frowned. 'We cleared everything away last night. Are you saying it's less than perfect?'

'Hah.' He made a choking sound. 'You're joking, aren't you? You can't see the floor in there for plastic, among other things, and it looks as though the new cushions have been used for some kind of pillow fight. How can three young people cause so much devastation?'

She pulled in a calming breath. 'To be fair, I don't think Caitlin would have had much to do with it.'

'Just the two of them, then…that's even worse! How do you live with all this chaos?'

'I'm not sure I do.' She shrugged vaguely. 'This is all new to me, too, you know.'

'Yes, of course it is. I just don't think I could ever live like this.' He looked beyond her to the window and the garden outside and exhaled sharply.

She could see the reason. One part of the

once perfect lawn was a quagmire, an unpleasant memento of last night's storm.

'That part of the garden is always getting waterlogged.' His mouth flattened and he looked down at his watch. 'I need to finish getting ready. I only came down for coffee—on second thoughts, I'll get it later.'

He obviously needed to get away for a while from the scenes of devastation all around him. 'I'll make it for you,' she said. 'Will you have it in here?'

'Uh...I don't think so. I need to sort some papers out for my briefcase. I'll be in the study. Thanks.'

She left the coffee on his desk a couple of minutes later and went to rummage through the cupboards to see what was available for breakfast. He wouldn't have time for anything much, she guessed, so she switched on the gas oven and started to heat up a batch of croissants. He hadn't meant what he'd said about not living like this, had he? Did he never want to have a family of his own?

She began to clear up the kitchen, wiping down the surfaces and mopping the floor, until it was restored to its former glory. The room was warm from the heat of the oven and her face was flushed from her exertions so after a while she undid a few buttons and ran a hand through her shoulder-length curls, pushing them back from her cheeks.

Leaving the children at the table, spooning jam on their croissants, she slid a couple more on to a plate and took them along to the study.

Tyler was in there, standing by the desk, sipping coffee while leafing through a stack of papers. His briefcase was open, next to his laptop bag, and it looked as though he had everything more or less in hand.

'I brought you these,' she said softly. 'You should eat something before you go.'

Perhaps she had taken him by surprise when she walked into the room. It may have been that he hadn't heard her knock or he was absorbed in what he was reading…whatever caused it, he suddenly seemed to swallow his coffee the wrong way and coughed, staring at her with a stunned expression. She had no idea what was wrong. All she knew was that his gaze never wavered from her and as he stood, as though mesmerised, the coffee started to spill from his cup in a slow, inevitable drip, drip onto his papers.

'Tyler, your coffee—'

He came to with a snap, putting his cup down and muttering something incomprehensible under his breath.

'Here, let me help.' She hurried forward, pulling some clean tissues out of a box on the table, but he put up a hand and warded her off.

'No…don't help me…don't do anything… please.' He gritted the words through his teeth. 'Just stay away…I can manage. Thank you.'

She didn't understand his rejection, and seeing his irritability she backed away from him, feeling hurt and awkward. Why could she never get anything right? Or, rather, why was nothing ever right for him where she was concerned?

'You know, Tyler,' she said carefully, 'you should start to think about what's most important in life. You can work towards making an awesome presentation, and you can live your life in a beautiful show house, but none of those things are important in the grand scheme of things. People are what matter…people who care for you and make it so that you want to come home to them. Perhaps you need to take some time to work out what it is you really want.'

He stared at her, straightening up from mopping up his damp papers. 'Saskia—'

'No, please don't say anything. I think you've already said enough. I'm going to leave you to get ready for your trip to the mainland. I hope everything goes well for you.'

She went back to the kitchen and tidied up, doing anything she could to keep busy and avoid him. She made sure that the children gathered up their belongings and returned the house to the way it had been when they'd arrived.

The power came back on a few minutes later as they left the house.

CHAPTER NINE

'WILL MUMMY AND Daddy be coming home soon?' Becky sat patiently on the edge of the bed on Sunday morning while Saskia brushed her hair. Her golden curls gleamed in the sunlight that filtered through the curtains.

'I hope so,' Saskia answered cautiously. 'Your mummy is feeling a lot better, so that's good news, isn't it? Perhaps we should get her some flowers and magazines, and maybe take some books in for your daddy to read?' Though whether he'd be feeling up to reading was up for debate at the moment.

'Yes. He likes detective stories.'

'Okay, we'll sort some out for him.'

Becky went off to play and Saskia sat for a while, thinking about everything that had happened in these last few weeks. It was as though she'd been caught up in a whirlwind that had tossed her this way and that.

And through it all there had been Tyler. She sighed. Did he even know how much he was missing out? Was it so important that everything be organised and carefully structured?

He'd been under stress yesterday—it had been the culmination of a long tense previous day and he'd been up into the early hours, getting things just right. It was no wonder he'd lost his cool. When he was under that kind of constant tension something was bound to give way. Even so, it hurt that he couldn't seem to get his priorities right.

Pulling herself together, she made her regular call to the hospital. Perhaps Sam would be feeling a bit better today. She could really do with some good news.

'I'm afraid he's taken a turn for the worse and we're really quite worried about him,' the nurse told her, and her spirits sank. 'We're doing everything we can to make him comfortable, but he's finding it difficult to get his breath. The doctor's coming in to see him some time this morning—fairly soon, we hope.'

Saskia cut the call after a minute or so and tried to think what she should do. She needed to go and see Sam, but it wouldn't be right to take the children with her when he was so ill. It would worry them too much.

There was only one thing to do…she would have to ask Tyler for help. She didn't want to do it, but she really didn't see any other way out. Rosie wouldn't be able to look after the children today and there was no one else she could call on.

She went downstairs to prepare breakfast for everyone and then left Caitlin in charge while she hurried next door.

'Saskia—it's good to see you.' Tyler invited her into the house, obviously a little puzzled because she was on her own. 'Have you left the children to their own devices? Are you sure the house is going to be safe from them while you're out?'

She managed a rueful smile. 'I'm sure everything will be fine for a few minutes.' She walked with him to the kitchen but turned down his offer of a cup of coffee. 'No, thanks. I can't stay.' She looked around. The place was spotless as usual.

'How did the presentation go yesterday?' she asked. 'It must have been good—you put a lot of work into it.'

He smiled. 'Yes, it went well, thanks. I think some changes will be made regionally now, based on our model for cardiovascular services.'

'A success, then.' Her mouthed tilted a fraction. 'I expect Imogen is pleased.'

'Yes, she is. She put a lot of effort into getting things right.'

'With your help.'

'Well, yes…we're friends, after all, so when she asked me for advice I did what I could for her.'

'You're just friends?'

Perhaps something in her voice implied she thought otherwise, because he said quietly, 'Yes, that's all. There's nothing going on between us.' He gave her a probing glance. 'Saskia, about yesterday—'

'It's all right. You don't need to explain.' It was a huge relief to have her mind put at rest on that score, but things had moved on and now she doubted she and Tyler could ever get together in the way she wanted. They were way too different in their outlook. As much as she loved him, she doubted it would ever work between them.

She said carefully, 'You were under a lot of stress. It was difficult for you, having us all invade your space, and then it seemed as though your hard work might be ruined at the last minute. I do understand.'

He shook his head. 'I don't think you do. I try to do my best, but somehow when I'm with you things never go according to plan.' He frowned. 'The trouble is, I can't think straight when I'm around you. I get distracted and I'm not usually like that. I've always been clear-headed and on the ball and it's frustrating not being in control any more.'

Her mouth quirked. 'So I'm to blame for your mistakes? Sorry, but it won't hold up in court.'

He laughed. 'You know what I mean.'

'I think so, yes.' She gave a rueful smile. She was glad he couldn't think straight around her—but it still worried her that they were miles apart in the way they lived their lives, and there was nothing on earth she could do to change that.

She frowned. 'Tyler, the reason I'm here… I came to ask a favour. I'm worried about Sam—there's been bad news from the hospital and I need to go and see him. The only thing is, I don't think it's a good idea to take the children with me, so—'

'You want me to look after them for you?'

She nodded anxiously. 'I know it's a lot to ask.'

'That's all right. They can come round here and hang out.'

She breathed a sigh of relief. 'Thanks. I didn't

know what else to do. They could watch DVDs if you want to make life easier on yourself… and Becky and Charlie can bring their colouring books. Those usually keep them quiet for half an hour or so. Caitlin's no trouble, of course. She'll sort herself out.'

'Don't worry about it.' He studied her face. 'Have you called the number I gave you to arrange a boat ride over there?'

'Not yet. I had to sort this out first.'

'Okay, I'll give Tim a ring for you. I'm sure he won't mind taking you over there and picking you up again later. He's Nicole's husband— he owes me a few favours.'

'Thanks. That'll be a great help, if he really is okay with it. I'd better go and organise things.' She made to turn away but he stopped her, laying a hand gently on her arm. For a second or two her heart gave a staccato beat, but he didn't take her into his arms or try to kiss her, and despondency made her shoulders droop a little.

'Have you taken your seasickness tablets?'

She pulled in a quick breath. 'No...I didn't give it a thought.' She winced. 'They won't work in time, will they?'

'I'll give you an injection. It'll make you a bit sleepy for about an hour, but you can curl up in a chair until Tim arrives, and he won't mind if you doze off on the boat. I'll explain things to him.'

She frowned. 'How is it that you have the right medication to hand? You can't keep everything in your medical bag, can you?'

'This is an island community, and people use boats quite a lot to get around. We're used to islanders and tourists having problems, so now we're prepared.' He waved her to a chair. 'Make yourself comfortable while I go and get things sorted out. I'll organise the children so all you need to do is rest and let the injection do its work.'

Half an hour later, feeling very drowsy, she was on the boat, heading for Cornwall. She only hoped that Tyler wouldn't regret agreeing to watch over the children. For a man who

craved peace and quiet and pleasant, tidy surroundings above all, it was a tall order.

'Give me a call when you want to go home,'
the boatman said when he eventually helped
her onto the towpath on the mainland. 'My
mate will see you the rest of the way. I hope everything works out all right for you with your
brother.'

'Thanks, Tim.'

Tim's friend was waiting to drive her to the
hospital, and she couldn't help thinking how
smooth the process was once Tyler had taken
a hand in the organisation.

Things were not so good when she arrived
at the hospital and went to Sam's ward. She
barely had time to say hello to him before a
team came to wheel him away towards the lift.
She looked at them in bewilderment. What was
going on? Sam was in pain and too breathless to talk so she simply squeezed his hand
and said softly, 'I'll wait. I'll be here when you
come back.'

'He's going to Theatre for a catheter embolectomy,' a nurse explained. 'He's very poorly. He had a chest pain that came on suddenly, stopping him from getting his breath, and his heart rate is very fast. We had to send for the doctor urgently and he took him to have a CTPA scan. I'm afraid it showed a blood clot on the lung.'

'Oh, no...' All at once Saskia was very afraid for her brother. The symptoms were ominous, given that Sam had been hospitalised for some length of time. Being stuck in bed could mean that the blood coagulated to form a clot in the deep vein of the leg and in Sam's case it had broken away and travelled through the heart to the lung, where it had stopped the blood from flowing freely. It was a terrifying event. The patient could collapse suddenly or even die.

Saskia reached for a chair and sat down, feeling very weak. The fact that they were doing a catheter embolectomy meant that the doctors felt he was in real danger. A fine tube would be passed through the blood vessels until it reached the clot and then the embolus would be carefully pulled out along the tube using specialist procedures.

'Can I get you anything?' the nurse asked. 'A cup of tea perhaps? That might help to make you feel a bit better.'

'Thanks.' Saskia was too worried to concentrate on anything properly. Her brother's life was at stake and she was helpless to do anything about it. Worse still, as a doctor she knew the risks involved.

Her mobile phone trilled and she went out into the corridor to answer it. It was a huge relief to hear Tyler's voice at the other end of the line.

'How's he doing?'

'It's not good.' She quickly told him what was happening. 'He's been really ill for the last couple of days and finally this morning the blood clot started to cause problems with his heart.'

'I'm so sorry, Saskia. I know you must be feeling awful right now...but at least they suspected what was happening and looked into it. Sometimes it's hard to know what's going on and these things can be missed. Sam's getting the treatment he needs.'

'I know. I just have to wait and hope and pray that he'll be all right.'

'He's in the best place for that kind of procedure. They have all the facilities they need and the surgeons are brilliant. He's in good hands.'

'Yes.' She tried to absorb all that and to allow his words to calm her. She said thoughtfully, 'How are things with you? Are you coping with the children? They're very quiet—I can't hear a sound from them in the background.'

'Ah, well, gags can do that. They're a very effective measure when you're desperate.'

'Tyler!' In spite of all her worries she laughed.

He chuckled. 'No, seriously, they're fine. We're getting along okay. I think we'll cope until you get back.'

She gave a sigh of relief. 'Good. That's one less worry, anyway. Thanks for doing this for me, Tyler.'

'You're welcome.'

They talked for a few more minutes and then

she cut the call. He'd managed to boost her spirits and he'd given her the strength to face up to what was happening with her brother.

She heard the rumble of a bed being wheeled back into the ward some time later, and straight away she stood up and went over to the bay where Sam was being treated.

He was drowsy and sedated, but he managed a smile. 'Hi, Sassie,' he said wearily. 'I'm glad you're still here. That was a bit scary, huh?'

'Too right,' she said, holding his hand in hers. 'How do you feel?'

'Tired…a bit sore…a whole lot better.'

'That's brilliant news.' She gave his hand a squeeze. 'You have to stop doing this to me, do you hear? You're to get better from now on and stop idling about in this bed. We want you back home.'

He smiled. 'I'll do my best.'

She gave him a hug and sat with him for some time until gradually his eyes closed and he fell into a deep, restful sleep.

'What happens now?' she asked the nurse. 'Has the doctor prescribed anticoagulants?'

'Yes, he has. He'll be on them for the next three months, I imagine.' She smiled. 'But I'm sure he'll be back home long before that. He should start to pick up from here on.'

Feeling much happier, and after a quick visit to Megan, Saskia set about making arrangements for her journey home. She was looking forward to seeing Tyler and the children, but her thoughts were tinged with apprehension. Would he really have been able to cope with the mess and noise and general disorder that three boisterous children could create? Why did she have to go and fall in love with someone who was the total opposite of herself?

Everything was quiet at first when she arrived back home later that afternoon. It was very odd. Boomer barked from somewhere in Tyler's house but no one came to answer her ring on the doorbell and she stood for a moment, wondering what she ought to do next. Then she heard childish laughter coming from

the garden and she went in search of everyone, following the path around the side of the
building.

Her eyes widened at the sight that met her.
Dressed in jeans and T-shirts, Becky and Charlie were on their knees in mud where the garden had been flooded during the storm. They
were wearing Wellington boots and gardening
gloves and were busy putting plants into the
ground under Tyler's supervision.

'Now, where did we say this one should go?'
Tyler asked. He, too, was on his knees. 'Oh, I
remember. Over there, where there's a space—
it'll look good won't it, with those red flowers
against the hosta in the background?'

Becky was studying the label. '"Late-flower-
ing primula",' she read. 'It smells nice, doesn't
it?'

Tyler sniffed the coppery-red blooms. 'You're
right, it does.'

Charlie heaped soil over the roots and patted it into place. Then he laughed, wriggling

about and waving his arms in the air as he sang, '"Another one bites the dust!"'

They all chuckled, and Caitlin, who was sitting at a table with a pad and pen, said, 'All right, here's the next one—Japanese water iris.' She consulted her pad. 'That one has to go next to the weigela.'

'Here we go, then.' Tyler handed the plant to Becky. 'Do you want to plant this one?'

'Yep, I do.'

Saskia stepped forward and Tyler glanced up. She was flabbergasted by the way Tyler and the little ones were happily ensconced knee deep in mud—Tyler, who preferred everything clean, neat and shipshape. She couldn't believe her eyes.

'Hi, you're back! That's great.' He stood up, brushing his hands along the length of his blue jeans to get rid of the worst of the dirt. He searched her face cautiously. 'How's Sam? How did the procedure go?'

'He's all right. Everything went really well, without a hitch. I think he's going to be okay.'

'That's fantastic.' He grinned as he moved towards her. 'I'd hug you if I wasn't so dirty.'

She looked him up and down, puzzlement in her green eyes. 'I can't believe what I'm seeing,' she said. 'You're grubby from head to toe, the children are filthy—how am I supposed to get their clothes clean after this?'

'They'll be fine. I told them to change into their oldest clothes. I'll shake the dirt off them and then we'll put them in the washing machine. No problem.'

She shook her head in disbelief. 'I would never have expected you to get involved in anything like this. I'm surprised Boomer isn't here with you, diving in among everybody.'

Tyler nodded. 'Oh, he tried. He kept wanting to help out with the digging, so in the end I had to put him back inside the house.' He waved a hand towards the area they were planting. 'What do you think of it?'

'I'm absolutely amazed,' she said. 'This is not like you at all. It's all curved edges and back to nature—there's nothing formal in it at all. You've actually dug up part of the lawn.'

'Well, it was always flooding, which made it difficult to maintain, and Caitlin caught me looking at it. She said, "Why don't you plant it with things that like a lot of moisture?" She's a clever girl, isn't she?'

Saskia nodded.

'So I took them all along to the garden centre and we picked out some plants that we thought might be good. And, hey, presto! It's done. Almost.'

'Good heavens.' She shook her head again. 'I can't get over it.'

His mouth curved briefly. 'Look, I need to go and take a quick shower. Why don't you stay here and see that they follow the plan Caitlin's drawn up, and I'll be back in two ticks?'

'Yes. I'll do that.'

He hurried away, leaving her to look around. She was stunned by everything that she'd seen. Tyler didn't do this sort of thing. He'd never had much to do with children and mess and what bit he had seen he hadn't liked. So this was a whole new aspect, something she had trouble taking on board. And the children were mud-spattered! Good grief.

He came back into the garden as she was helping Caitlin identify a pretty plant with pink flowers and spiky foliage. He'd given her a sitting-down job because she was supposed to be convalescing. '"Hesperantha",' she said, reading the label. 'It's not one I'm familiar with.'

'I've made some tea,' Tyler announced. He was fresh and clean, wearing chinos and a shirt open at the neck, and he looked good, so different from the way he'd looked just a short time ago. Still, even grimy, he'd had an air of devil-may-care sexiness about him. 'Do you children want to finish off now, and then go and get cleaned up?' he said. 'You can leave your wellies in the utility room.'

'I'll see to it that they tidy up,' Caitlin said. 'We've about finished here, anyway.'

'That's good. Thanks. You've all done a brilliant job.'

He went with Saskia back to the kitchen and she stood by the table, simply staring at him. 'This is such an earth-shattering event,' she said, 'you throwing off your inhibitions and getting mixed up with we ordinary, untidy mortals. I can't get used to it.'

'Don't you like it?'

She smiled. 'I love it. I'm just wondering whether it will last. I mean, people don't change, do they?'

'Not usually, maybe.' He came over to her and put his arms around her. 'I'm glad your brother's all right—your sister-in-law, too,' he said. 'Perhaps now you'll be able to relax and look forward to the future.'

'Yes. It's a good feeling.' It was heavenly having his arms around her. She wanted to rest her head against his chest and feel the beat of his heart beneath her cheek, but would things turn out the way she hoped? Dared she believe in a future where Tyler was there for her, come what may?

'I thought about what you said,' he told her.

'Ever since I was little I've longed for stability and security, but it was always elusive. The only way I could control what happened in my life was to make everything around me structured, methodical, neat and tidy. That was the only thing I felt I had any influence over.'

His hands stroked gently along her spine. 'And then, after you told me I should think about what was important, I realised that I was letting the most vital, essential part of my life slip away…you. I was pushing you away.' He lifted his hand to her cheek and lightly trailed his finger over the line of her jaw. 'I couldn't bear to have you leave me,' he said huskily. 'I want you above all else, Saskia. I love you. I'd do anything for you.'

A soft, shuddery sigh escaped her. 'That's all I ever wanted to hear, Tyler…that you love me. I fell in love with you against all my instincts, all my fears that everything would go wrong. But I know now that you're the only man I could ever truly love.'

A muffled groan of relief rumbled in his chest and he hugged her close to him, kissing her deeply, fervently, holding her as though he would never let her go.

'I can change,' he whispered against her cheek. 'For you, I'll do it…and it won't be a hardship. It'll be a new beginning.'

'You don't have to do anything,' she said. 'I'm sure we'll work things out—as long as we have each other, everything will come right.'

'It will if you say you'll marry me,' he said, his voice roughened. 'Will you marry me, Saskia? You'll make me the happiest man on earth if you say yes.'

'Yes,' she said, smiling up at him. 'I will.'

His breath caught in his throat. 'You've made my life full, brought me so much warmth and love and shown me what I've been missing. As long as I have you I could never ask for anything more. I'll never let you down.'

'I know you won't,' she said. 'I love you. From now on we'll be together and life is going to be good, so good.'

She lifted her face for his kiss, and for the next age they were lost in one another. It felt as though she'd come home.

* * * * *

MILLS & BOON®
Large Print Medical

March

A SECRET SHARED...   Marion Lennox
FLIRTING WITH THE DOC OF HER DREAMS   Janice Lynn
THE DOCTOR WHO MADE HER LOVE AGAIN   Susan Carlisle
THE MAVERICK WHO RULED HER HEART   Susan Carlisle
AFTER ONE FORBIDDEN NIGHT...   Amber McKenzie
DR PERFECT ON HER DOORSTEP   Lucy Clark

April

IT STARTED WITH NO STRINGS...   Kate Hardy
ONE MORE NIGHT WITH HER DESERT PRINCE... Jennifer Taylor
FLIRTING WITH DR OFF-LIMITS   Robin Gianna
FROM FLING TO FOREVER   Avril Tremayne
DARE SHE DATE AGAIN?   Amy Ruttan
THE SURGEON'S CHRISTMAS WISH   Annie O'Neil

May

PLAYING THE PLAYBOY'S SWEETHEART   Carol Marinelli
UNWRAPPING HER ITALIAN DOC   Carol Marinelli
A DOCTOR BY DAY...   Emily Forbes
TAMED BY THE RENEGADE   Emily Forbes
A LITTLE CHRISTMAS MAGIC   Alison Roberts
CHRISTMAS WITH THE MAVERICK MILLIONAIRE   Scarlet Wilson

MILLS & BOON®
Large Print Medical

June

MIDWIFE'S CHRISTMAS PROPOSAL	Fiona McArthur
MIDWIFE'S MISTLETOE BABY	Fiona McArthur
A BABY ON HER CHRISTMAS LIST	Louisa George
A FAMILY THIS CHRISTMAS	Sue MacKay
FALLING FOR DR DECEMBER	Susanne Hampton
SNOWBOUND WITH THE SURGEON	Annie Claydon

July

HOW TO FIND A MAN IN FIVE DATES	Tina Beckett
BREAKING HER NO-DATING RULE	Amalie Berlin
IT HAPPENED ONE NIGHT SHIFT	Amy Andrews
TAMED BY HER ARMY DOC'S TOUCH	Lucy Ryder
A CHILD TO BIND THEM	Lucy Clark
THE BABY THAT CHANGED HER LIFE	Louisa Heaton

August

A DATE WITH HER VALENTINE DOC	Melanie Milburne
IT HAPPENED IN PARIS...	Robin Gianna
THE SHEIKH DOCTOR'S BRIDE	Meredith Webber
TEMPTATION IN PARADISE	Joanna Neil
A BABY TO HEAL THEIR HEARTS	Kate Hardy
THE SURGEON'S BABY SECRET	Amber McKenzie